D0371636

Becca Fair and Foul

Becca Fair and Foul

Deirdre Baker

Groundwood Books / House of Anansi Press
Toronto Berkeley

Groundwood Books / House of Anansi Press
groundwoodbooks.com

We acknowledge for their financial support of our publishing program the Canada
Council for the Arts, the Ontario Arts Council and the Government of Canada.

 Canada Council   Conseil des Arts
for the Arts   du Canada

 ONTARIO ARTS COUNCIL
CONSEIL DES ARTS DE L'ONTARIO
an Ontario government agency
un organisme du gouvernement de l'Ontario

With the participation of the Government of Canada | Canadä
Avec la participation du gouvernement du Canada

Library and Archives Canada Cataloguing in Publication
Baker, Deirdre F. (Deirdre Frances), author
Becca fair and foul / Deirdre Baker.
Issued in print and electronic formats.
ISBN 978-1-55498-957-7 (hardcover). — ISBN 978-1-55498-959-1 (HTML).
— ISBN 978-1-55498-960-7 (Kindle)
I. Title.
PS8603.A455B45 2018   jC813'.6   C2017-905948-3
C2017-905949-1

Jacket design by Michael Solomon
Jacket art by Julianna Swaney

Groundwood Books is committed to protecting our natural environment.
As part of our efforts, the interior of this book is printed on paper that contains
100% post-consumer recycled fibers, is acid-free and is processed chlorine-free.

Printed and bound in Canada

MIX
Paper from
responsible sources
FSC® C016245
www.fsc.org

All torment, trouble, wonder and amazement
inhabits here.
The Tempest, Act V, Scene 1

for Robin, Lily and Ariel

1. Seabird

~~~~~~

"WE NEED a better boat," said Becca.

Gull was slow. She was cracked and she clanged in the waves because she was made of aluminum.

Even with a clumsy boat, sailing was good, but what would it be like to sail in a ship really made to fly? One in which she and Jane could sail away, have adventures and come home when they were good and ready?

"Shift to port," she told Jane.

The sail flapped as if it hadn't quite woken up yet, and Becca sailed *Gull* out of Gran's bay.

But it was more like crawling than flying.

"What's wrong with *Gull*?" Jane asked.

"Uncle Martin and Auntie Meg say she sails like a gumboot."

"Like a gumboot chiton?" Jane laughed, because gumboot chitons were sea creatures that stuck onto rocks and never went anywhere much.

"Just a regular gumboot," Becca said. "A wellie. A rubber boot. That's what Auntie Meg said."

And for a moment she remembered last summer, and Auntie Meg singing sea shanties and rowing through mountainous seas.

"Where should we go?" asked Jane. "How about Seal Rock?"

"Yes, Seal Rock!" said Becca. "The tide's on the ebb. We'll see if there are any seals there today."

"We learned about sailing in school," Jane said. "We did a play about a shipwreck. It was called *The Tempest.*"

Becca thought it was joyless of Jane to mention shipwreck when it was the first voyage of summer and the first time she and Jane were allowed to go to sea without an adult. Shipwreck would wreck not just *Gull* but everything — all their plans for sailing around the island, if only they could get permission.

"I phoned Dugald this morning —"

"Uncle Mac," corrected Jane. Her great-uncle Dugald Macallan was a local weatherman, and it was often his voice that they heard on the recorded weather announcement. "And it must have been a substitute Dugald," she added, "because Uncle Mac's here."

"He's talking to Merlin about waterworks," Becca said.

It was Gran who called it waterworks. But it was just plumbing, which is what Merlin did when he wasn't in a boat, or fighting fires, or arguing with Aunt Fifi if she happened to be visiting Gran.

"Well," said Jane. "What did substitute Dugald say?"

"Boring. Northwest winds, ten to fifteen knots."

Diminishing to five to ten knots, Dugald had added. That was hardly any wind at all. They'd be lucky to get anywhere.

"Why don't you let me have a go?" asked Jane. "Maybe something interesting will happen."

"Something interesting" is just what Gran had told Becca she didn't want to happen when she gave Becca permission to sail *Gull* out of the bay. Gran was remembering something Mum and Auntie Clare had done a long time ago and said she wasn't going to go through that again and neither were the neighbors.

"You're the skipper," Gran had said. "You have to take responsibility for all decisions or you'll lose your job. So put that in your pipe and smoke it."

But Becca couldn't see what could go wrong on a day as quiet as this.

*   *   *

Jane was fine at sailing, if you could call it that with the sail hanging so limp. *Gull* slowed to a pace so listless that Becca almost fell asleep.

Far in the hot sunny distance she could see someone trudging across the seaweedy beach to Seal Rock.

"Look!" she said. "Someone's going to beat us there."

You could only walk to Seal Rock at the lowest of low tides. Humans didn't go there usually, but today the tide was almost as far out as it ever got. The seals would be bothered and swim away, Becca thought, with a human poking around.

"*Gull* isn't even a gumboot," said Jane.

"More like a geographical feature," said Becca, remembering certain books she had read. "Like a lump, or a boulder, or an ancient Viking ship fossilized with the remains of a noble warrior because Vikings loved to fight and then get buried in their ships in a hill."

Gull crept onwards.

"A geological pace," said Becca. "That's what Aunt Fifi would say. She'd hate this. She likes to move fast."

But they were getting there. Now Becca could see Seal Rock's special boulder, the one that looked like a tortoise from some angles. And there was a bump on it, so maybe there were still seals there.

"The tide's turned," she said. She could feel the change in the sea's flow.

Such as it was.

She hung over the gunwales. She saw red and purple sea urchins waving their spines. She saw sea cucumbers, sluggish on the sea's floor, and sun stars, bright as sunset and rosy as dawn, tiptoeing this way and that on their many legs and hundreds of tiny sucker-feet.

The sun stars were moving faster than *Gull.*

* * *

"We're there," Jane said at last. That was after they had drunk their ginger beer and Jane had laughed some of hers out her nose, and they had eaten most of Gran's scary cheese-and-onion sandwiches.

It was after the tide had made Seal Rock back into an island.

They pulled *Gull* up and walked around the islet, trying not to pay attention to the person on tortoise rock. For it was a person, not a seal, they could see now that they were there.

But there were no seals. Not one.

"They were here, though," said Jane.

There were fishy remains everywhere, and clumps of old fur all brown and tufty. There was gray crumbly stuff, too, that Becca didn't want to know too much about.

"I think this is where seal babies hang out," Jane said.

"Look at this hunk of fur!"

"Oh!" said Jane. "It still has skin on it."

"Even the air is nourishing," Becca said. She thought it must be at least as good for you as those awful fish-oil capsules they sold in vitamin stores.

"If you can stand it."

"Take your hand off your nose. I can't understand you," said Becca.

There was a snorty, croaking noise from tortoise rock, and the person there sat up.

"It's just seal and sea-lion leavings," he said. "Old meals and a little poop."

"Merlin!" Becca exclaimed. "What are you doing here?"

"I thought you were talking with Uncle Mac," said Jane.

"I was," said Merlin. "And then I went for a walk."

"Did you come here to talk to the seals?" asked Jane.

"I came to be alone."

"How can you be alone?" asked Becca. "Don't you have a pager or something?"

"I turned it off," Merlin said. "A person needs a little peace now and then." He closed his eyes. "Feel free to ignore me."

Becca and Jane went on exploring.

"Look! A seal tooth!" Jane exclaimed.

"I didn't know seals lost their teeth," Becca said. "Is there a tooth fairy for seals?"

"I can't sleep with you girls clonking about," Merlin declared, sitting up again.

"Come help us finish our sandwiches," said Becca.

They sat against lumpy tortoise rock.

"Who made these?" Merlin asked, when his eyes had stopped running with onion tears. "They're very aggressive sandwiches."

"Gran," said Becca. "She calls these onions sweet and says they taste like apples."

"Apples!" Merlin blew more onion tears out his nose.

"What time is it?" he suddenly asked. "I'd better be going."

"But you can't," Becca said.

For the sea had been coming in quickly and serenely, creeping up the shore. Already it felt like Seal Rock was shrinking, sinking quietly into the strait, perhaps preparing to become the seals' nighttime bedroom once more.

Well, not really. Becca didn't really think seals slept here, but she pointed to the water swelling up around the islet.

Merlin jumped to his feet and clambered over the cobbles and conglomerate, up over the driftwood, dried grasses and prickly plants. He leapt towards the distant beach as if — if he moved fast enough — he'd be able to soar across the widening channel between Seal Rock and the island.

But even a deer in full flight couldn't have leapt so far.

"Ow!"

There was a tumbling, knocking sound, and a sea-lionish noise from Merlin.

"Ow!" he repeated. "That log rolled away right under my feet."

Becca and Jane looked at him. He was sitting in a pile of smelly fur, clutching his ankle.

"Can you walk?" Becca asked.

"I don't know," Merlin said. "But it's all right. It'll be better in a while."

"We can't leave you marooned here," Becca said.

"And wounded," said Jane.

"I don't need rescuing!"

"You can't stay here all night," Becca said. "And even if you could swim across, how would you get back home?"

"I'll be fine," Merlin said. "Ow."

"There's no point wiggling your ankle," Jane said. "It won't get better if you don't rest it."

"RICE," Becca told him. "Rest, ice, compression, elevation. That's what the aunts would say."

"Would you really stay here all night?" Jane asked.

It seemed like a long time for Merlin to sit on a rock in the sea — all evening and all night, too, because the night tide wouldn't be low enough for someone to get across without swimming a long way.

And swimming in the dark alone was a bad idea.

"I could work it out eventually," Merlin sighed. "But I'm supposed to be somewhere this evening. And Mrs. Barker's pressure pump needs attention."

*   *   *

Becca and Jane lifted *Gull* into the sea.

"Welcome aboard," said Jane. "Watch out for the boom."

"Can you swim?" Becca asked.

"Of course I can swim!" Merlin answered.

"That's good," Becca said, "because we don't have a spare life jacket."

Gull sank a little as he climbed in.

"Ow!" he cried, and fell over the centerboard.

"Push off as hard as you can, Becca," said Jane. "We need all the momentum we can get."

Becca gave *Gull* a great shove and hopped aboard.

"Don't you have oars?" Merlin asked.

Becca thought of the oars standing at attention against the shed, waiting for her to bring them down and put them in *Gull* just in case they were needed. Which they were, in this windless world, and what a pity she and Jane had forgotten them.

Or, if she was really the skipper, *she* had forgotten them.

And now she was allowing a life-jacketless passenger aboard as well.

But what else could she do?

*   *   *

The sea spread out around them, a mirror for blue sky and summer heat. Its only motion was the slow underwater surge of incoming tide.

And there was no doubt about it, Becca thought, as time drifted by. Oars would have been handy.

"We're not *so* far out," she said.

"They can probably see us with binoculars," said Jane.

"They didn't say anything about the naked eye," Becca said.

"Are you in trouble?" asked Merlin.

"Not yet," Becca said. "What if we whistle for a wind? Would that work?"

"We could sing," Jane suggested. "It's more breathy."

The boom swayed with lazy twitches, and Merlin cleared his throat.

"How about a sea shanty?" he asked. *"Betsy had a baby and she dressed it all in white ..."*

"Heave away, Johnny, all bound to go," Jane joined in.

Becca listened.

"The tide came in one morning and it crept up to the door ... It took that little baby and 'twas never seen no more ... Heave away, Johnny, all bound to go ..."

Becca's skin shivered. She didn't know why. Maybe it was Merlin — he had a clear, soaring voice. She never would have guessed that he could sound like that, looking at his dirty T-shirt and grubby jeans, his freckly face and his teeth that, she remembered, might clack at any moment because some of them were false.

The song reminded Becca of something, but she couldn't think what while she was worried about getting her ship and crew and passenger back home to harbor.

"We're not leaving," she said. "There's the whole summer! Can't you think of an arriving song?"

Becca saw a ripple feather the water, but it vanished almost at once and the water went sleek again. Gran's bay seemed farther off than ever.

"I really do have to be somewhere this evening," Merlin said. "Even though Mrs. Barker can probably wait for her pressure pump. Can't we hurry up?"

Becca waggled the tiller.

"We could be engines," she said. "We could hang onto the stern and kick."

She tried not to imagine what Gran would say about that, or Mum or Dad, or Mac, or Jane's parents, or any other friend or relative.

"Can you sail?" she asked Merlin. "Could you steer, if Jane and I get out and kick?"

"We're going to be motors?" asked Jane.

"We have life jackets and our legs work. We can push the boat."

"I can sail," Merlin said. "I mean, I probably can — with no wind."

"You don't have a life jacket, so you can't be a man overboard," said Becca. "And anyway, kicking would hurt your ankle. You can steer and sing. Maybe it will raise a wind."

"Aye, aye, sir," said Merlin.

* * *

"One, two, three!"

Becca and Jane pushed *Gull*, and then they kicked hard to catch up to her.

Then they pushed again.

There went Mayfield Point, so slowly that Becca had time to count its trees, to think she could see where snoozing deer had flattened the grasses.

There went the pebbly beach where Becca's baby sister, Pin, liked to throw rocks into the sea or sometimes try to eat them.

Merlin sang a song about a father lying under five fathoms of ocean. *"Of his bones are coral made,"* he sang. *"Those are pearls that were his eyes."*

"Don't you know any cheerful songs?" Becca panted.

There was the point that wasn't really a point. Two eagles standing on the beach stared. And stared. Then finally, Becca couldn't see them anymore.

"My legs are numb," said Jane.

Becca memorized every pockmark on *Gull*'s stern.

Merlin sang about a cowslip's bell and then about flying on a bat.

It was getting harder to catch up with *Gull* after each push.

And now Becca's life jacket was giving her a rash, and her arms were stretching out longer and longer.

She watched a knot of kelp rise and fall, rise and fall. It passed by glittering with sun and sea, splattering drops that bounced up, then flew out over the water. Right behind it came a piece of driftwood, bobbing cheerfully like a tiny boat, much more lively than *Gull*.

There was something funny about that, but Becca was too tired to wonder.

Kick, kick, kick. Push, push, push.

Merlin's voice flew out above them, all about how there was a lover and his lass that through the green corn fields did pass.

"The water's green-looking," Jane said.

That's when Becca saw that the sea had changed.

"And it's sticking up like — like waves!"

But before Becca could say how puffs of wind were whipping up bits of sea, Merlin sang a sudden, great "Hey!" and *Gull* bounded ahead with a rush and a clang, surged forward like she could hardly wait to get home.

The sail flapped and snapped and bellied out, and the wind pushed, and *Gull* slammed on in the now-bouncing waves of the strait.

Merlin shouted, and Becca could feel *Gull* pulling away, galloping out from under her cramped hands. And there were Jane's fingers, stretching, stretching so that they had gone white and bloodless, because she could hardly hold onto *Gull*'s stern.

"I'm going to have to let go!" shouted Jane. "She's going too fast!"

"Kick!" Becca yelled. "Let out the sheet! Spill the wind!"

"Sheet?" asked Merlin. "What sheet?"

Gull tore herself from Becca's fingers. Becca swam frantically. The bulky life jacket dragged at her arms.

All Becca could see was *Gull*'s wake, the small turmoil of sea gurgling behind her. And *Gull*'s stern, speeding farther and farther away from Becca's reaching arms.

Then, quite by accident, Merlin shifted the tiller. The sail emptied and *Gull* lost momentum.

"Get in," Becca said, and she shoved Jane over the stern.

"Take my hand," Merlin said, and in a moment, Becca was safe by the tiller.

"It happened so fast!" said Jane.

"We weren't paying attention," said Merlin.

"I wasn't," Becca said. And she should have been, she thought. She was the skipper.

She thought of the feel of her fingers, of *Gull* slipping away from them.

She thought of Jane's hand hooked onto *Gull* by its fingertips. She thought of the great broad strait with its muscular flow.

It wasn't even very windy. Just a little frisk, really, enough to get them to Jane's point in time for dinner maybe.

But for a moment, *Gull* had been about to sail off without them.

What would be worse than wrecking *Gull*?

Becca and Jane, lost at sea.

* * *

DEIRDRE BAKER

"Muscles on them like Olympic swimmers!"

That was Mac's greeting as *Gull* was hauled ashore by Gran, Mac, Jane's mum, Jane's dad and even Bill-and-Kay-next-door who happened to be standing on the point with their binoculars when Becca finally sailed *Gull* up to the sandstone.

"And who's this?" asked Gran. "Merlin! Where's your life jacket?"

"Why didn't you row?" asked Mac.

"What were you doing out there?" Jane's mum asked.

"What's wrong with your foot?" asked Mac.

"You know better than to go to sea without a life jacket," said Gran. "Don't you?"

"They saved me," Merlin said. "I didn't mean to go to sea."

"He was marooned," Becca said.

"And wounded," said Jane.

"We could barely spot you," said Mac. "I had to get out the telescope."

"Why were you overboard in the middle of the strait?" asked Jane's dad.

"Don't you realize *Gull* could have sailed off and left you?" Gran asked.

"We were becalmed," said Becca.

"It wasn't our fault," said Jane.

But it was, Becca knew. She was the skipper and she forgot the oars, and then she didn't stay close enough to shore to get home easily without them. And she took on a passenger she didn't have a life jacket for, and she let *Gull* drift way

{22}

out into the current. And then she jumped out of the boat and left it under the control of a person who didn't know a thing about sailing.

She thought about that moment when *Gull* had been about to escape them.

Those are pearls that were his eyes, Merlin had sung. *Full fathom five thy father lies.*

At least it wasn't us full fathom five, she thought.

"This is not good," said Jane's mum.

"Yes, it's serious," said Gran. "What an escapade! Becca, I think you'd better be beached for the time being unless you're with an adult."

"Merlin's an adult!" Becca said.

"Yes, well, someone who knows something about boats. You did well in some ways, but you and Jane aren't ready to sail on your own."

So that was that. The first day of summer. Beached.

2. Night Visitors

~~~~~~

"Beached!" Becca said. "We might as well have been wrecked!"

"We can always *walk* around the island," said Jane.

"But we wanted to spend the summer at sea!"

It had been a tiny miscalculation, Becca thought. A little mistake. Not an "escapade."

Even if *Gull* was sort of seaworthy, and even if some day they were allowed to go to sea again without an adult, they needed a better boat. Twice *Gull* had needed engines. Once last year with Auntie Meg and Uncle Martin when it had been too windy, and now with Jane because it hadn't been windy enough.

They kept having to use arms and legs to get anywhere — rowing and kicking.

"It's no good having a boat that's so tricky," she said.

She had carried her sleeping bag up to Jane's cabin on the point. The atmosphere around Gran's was rather prickly right now, what with no life jackets, forgotten oars and people overboard in the middle of the strait. A sleepover at Jane's was only sensible.

"We'll sleep on the beach," said Jane. "Then there won't be adults bossing us around."

"We should earn money and buy our own boat," Becca said. "But how?"

"I'm reading a book about kids who go to a dance school," said Jane. "They get paid for performing."

"Nobody's going to hire me to dance," Becca said. She hated dancing. She'd rather turn the compost for weeks than dance even for a minute.

"Here's a good place." Jane put her sleeping bag down in a hollow in the sandstone above the tide line. "It's like a bedroom."

The sandstone was dark there, and decorated with silver lichen. It curled up around a flat little floor of yellow grasses and it all made a cozy nook.

Becca lay down. There was just enough room for two mats and sleeping bags, and they'd be out of the wind. The tufty grasses were soft under her, and warm, too, as if they kept in their heads and stalks the sunshine that had dried them out.

"We could make bracelets and earrings to sell in the market," she said.

"But I'm terrible at that doodad stuff." Jane reached into her pillow case and tossed a bag of chips to Becca. "Salt and vinegar."

Then she rooted in her sleeping bag.

"Ginger beer."

"I wondered what the clanking was," Becca said, and she swigged heartily while Jane tore open the chips.

"Yo-ho-ho and a bottle of beer," said Jane, and they clinked bottles.

"To a new ship," toasted Becca.

On one side of the point, Midshipman Bay lay still and silvery, a couple of motor boats lying at anchor in its basin. Becca could see and hear the strait lapping at the shore on the other side of the point, still calm but alive somehow, with its silent current. The Inside Passage, it was called. The Salish Sea.

It was like being at sea without being at sea, having water on both sides of them.

The sunset bloomed pink and orange, and the grasses became dark silhouettes in the twilight. They drank the ginger beer and closed up half the chips for later.

It felt good to lie down after the long day.

And the thistles weren't so much of a problem. They were spiky and tall but grew out of a crack off to the side.

"I always wanted to sleep with my face in a blackberry vine," Jane said.

"My pillow's in a wild rose bush," said Becca.

"We won't notice once we fall asleep."

"And there won't be slugs because we're practically on the beach."

The grass smelled sweet and healthy, and the lichen on the sandstone did, too. There was another smell Becca couldn't identify, though it reminded her of something.

"We could mow lawns to make money," she said. "We could catch fish."

"Nobody has a lawn around here," said Jane. "And why

would they pay for fish they can catch themselves? What about babysitting?"

"Babysitting's part of my chores," Becca said.

Her sister, Pin, was too small to get into real trouble. She didn't have escapades yet, but she crawled around a lot, put everything in her mouth and wanted to hold onto things so she could stand up.

"Would they pay you if you looked after her for a whole day?" Jane wondered.

"Maybe. But we need more than that to buy a boat. And anyway, Mum and Dad and Pin aren't coming for weeks. Listen — it's calm again. You can hardly hear the sea."

They could hear the tiniest of waves stroking the beach. The sandpipers and killdeers whistled their goodnights. They made Becca think of sea songs.

"That was funny, hearing Merlin sing," she said.

Merlin had a pretty good voice — a fabulous voice, really. And so did Jane.

"You sounded good together," Becca told her.

"Maybe I could busk," Jane said.

"Where could you busk on this island?"

"At the ferry slip?"

"But it could take years to earn enough!"

Even an old, cheap, tiny sailing dinghy would cost a few hundred dollars.

It was almost dark now. Becca looked up at the Big Dipper and Cassiopeia and wondered why she still hadn't learned any more constellations. It was such a muddle up there.

She tried to find the North Star by using the lip of the Big Dipper. The North Star wasn't bright, she knew, but it was the important one, the one that didn't change. The rest wheeled around it every night.

It made her think of something Aunt Fifi had quoted once. "A star to every wandering bark," she had said. Aunt Fifi had explained that bark was an old word for ship, and the star was the way the sailor figured out where his ship was.

There was a ship, and a star, and it was a poem about love. Shakespeare, of course. Something Merlin and Aunt Fifi liked to argue about.

"Look!" Jane said. "A shooting star!"

*   *   *

When Becca woke, the sky was white with stars. But starlight wasn't what had woken her.

A noise had woken her. A noise so close, so real, that her heart shook her whole body with its terrified thumps.

Someone was there — or someones. She could hear them moving around, treading on the grasses and snapping sticks.

And they were talking!

She didn't dare say a word. What if they heard her? Who were they?

"Becca?" whispered Jane.

Whoever it was stopped. There was silence, and only the sound of Becca's own fear in her ears. She could feel Jane clutching her through the sleeping bag.

The someones moved again. They chattered, but they

weren't speaking English. It was some new language, a language that sounded partly like water burbling downhill, and partly like plates clattering in a river. There were snorts in it, and chewing noises.

Whoever they were, they were coming closer. They were coming right towards Becca and Jane, who were snuggled in their sleeping bags in the grass and the thistles and blackberry vines and wild rose bushes because with all those thorns and prickles, why would anyone disturb them?

They were sleeping there because the point was a good place, and if they needed adults, which was never likely, they could holler up to Jane's cabin.

But now the night was full of the cold light of stars, and strangers were coming, and Becca had never felt less like hollering. Or in fact like making any noise whatsoever.

Could it be Lucy and Alicia, Becca's trouble-making cousins? But they weren't supposed to arrive until tomorrow.

Every moment the noisemakers got closer. And there were more of them. They seemed to be multiplying.

It definitely wasn't Lucy and Alicia. It sounded like a whole party now and their talking was louder, full of churring and nose-clearing sounds, and consonants and vowels that were incomprehensible.

And they smelled of fish. They stank, really. The smell was a cloud hanging low in the night, weighing on Becca and forcing her head into her sleeping bag.

Whoever these fish-breathers were, they didn't know Becca and Jane were there.

Maybe, just maybe, she and Jane could scare them away.

Slowly, slowly, Becca turned her head and whispered right into Jane's ear. She reached down into her sleeping bag where she had hidden her headlamp, and then Jane whispered, "Now!"

They sat up and turned on their lights.

"Arf!" barked Jane. "Rrrruff rrrruff, arf-arf-arf, grrrrrrrr! Rrrruff!"

"Yip! Yip! Yip! Arp-arp! Grrrrrrr!" Becca growled.

Whiskery faces, dark eyes, round ears, wet fur sticking up all sporty and sharp — that's what Becca saw in that instant.

And at the same time she knew what the smell reminded her of — the rich smells of Seal Rock, with its seal-leavings, fish bones and fur and all sorts of half-digested marine life.

And now here was a whole family of river otters — more than a family, with mum and dad and aunts, uncles, cousins, grandparents, sisters, brothers and babies all crowded around her and Jane.

Who's sleeping in *my* bed? they seemed to be asking.

She and Jane shouldn't be here, Becca thought. But they were, and what were the otters going to do next?

"Rrrruff! Rrruff!" Jane growled. "Arf-arf-arf!"

The otters didn't say a word more. Their foreign speech went silent. In the light of the headlamps there was a quick writhing of long strong tails, of sleek short-legged bodies tumbling one over another.

They were gone.

"We stole their bedroom," Becca said, her heart whacking inside her so she could hardly breathe.

"The deck," squeaked Jane, hoarse from barking. "We don't have to wake up mum and dad. We can move to the deck."

*   *   *

They were back to looking for shooting stars.

"I wish I hadn't dropped my pillow in a tidepool," said Jane. "There's one!"

"We shouldn't have tried to carry everything at once," Becca said. "And my arms are all scratched from getting out in the middle of that rose bush."

"I'm hungry."

"We left the chips down there."

"I'm not going back to get them," said Jane.

"Me neither," Becca answered. "Anyway, the otters will like them. Fish and chips. What could be better?"

3. A Sickening Feeling

~~~~~~

IN THE MORNING, Becca's night thoughts were all mixed together — stars, poems, otters, sails, fish and chips, and ships on the beach.

Shakespeare.

"We'll put on a play," she said even before her eyes opened.

"And the play can be *The Tempest*!" said Jane. "There's a magician who bosses everyone around, and a lot of storminess and shipwreck, and in the end they get their ship back. It's about the sea and an island."

"That makes it perfect for raising money for a boat," Becca said. "And we won't even have to make a set because we're already on an island."

"There's a sprite and a monster-fish-man, and a magician who says, 'our little lives are rounded with a sleep,'" said Jane.

With her upsticking hair, rumpled pajamas and sleep-crusty eyes, Becca thought Jane looked perfect for the line.

"Your cousins can be in it," Jane said.

"Lucy and Alicia," said Becca. "They're coming today."

But she didn't think they cared about boats. And would they want to be in a play?

"It was a lot of work when we did it in school," said Jane. "But fun, too."

"And anyway, we're beached," said Becca, "so we might as well do something."

*　*　*

Lucy and Alicia arrived with Aunt Fifi.

"I told you not to pack a jar of marmalade with your clothes," Alicia said, climbing out of Aunt Fifi's sporty car.

"Well, I didn't expect you to hurl my backpack onto the ferry deck," said Lucy. "It's awful! My favorite shirt!"

She picked a few pieces of orange peel out of her backpack and ate them.

"Did the jar break?" Becca asked. "Isn't there glass in it?"

"The lid wasn't screwed on properly," Lucy told her. "Probably Alicia's fault."

"Not my fault! But definitely my fault the restaurant food spilled. And it was my favorite kind of chicken salad, too," mourned Alicia. "Luckily we finished off most of it while we were waiting for the ferry."

There must have been avocado in it, to make that green splodge on her shorts.

"My car will never forget it," Aunt Fifi remarked. "And, no, Becca, I didn't bring any Shakespeare this time. Maybe Merlin has a copy of *The Tempest*."

Gran turned to Lucy and Alicia, then seemed to change her mind about hugging their marmalade and chicken salad stains. She gave them each a little kiss on the cheek instead.

"Shakespeare!" Alicia said. "What would you want to do that for? It's school stuff. Ew."

And she pounded off down the trail with Lucy at her heels.

Why couldn't she and Lucy and Alicia be like mum and the aunts? Becca wondered. Whenever Mum and Aunt Fifi and Auntie Meg and Auntie Clare and Aunt Cat got together, they hugged each other and talked and talked and talked — as if they actually liked each other.

She picked up the wheelbarrow handles. An aunt, a gran and two cousins — and she still had to barrow the luggage herself.

*   *   *

After dinner Aunt Fifi went for a walk, or so she said. Whether she wanted to enjoy the scenery, look for Merlin or avoid Scrabble, Becca wasn't sure.

"Come, granddaughters," said Gran. "It's time for Scrabble."

"But —" Alicia protested.

"No buts," said Gran. "It's good for the brain." She carried the Scrabble game down to the beach in front of the cabin.

Becca was suddenly glad Lucy and Alicia were there. She didn't want to play Scrabble with Gran on her own. And it wasn't the right time to talk to them about putting on a play to raise money for a boat she and Jane wanted, but maybe playing Scrabble would put them in the mood.

Doing a play, even a long Shakespeare one, would be less work than playing Scrabble with Gran.

"It isn't so much the letters you get as what you do with them," Gran said after Lucy put down a six-letter word and only got a measly six points.

"All my letters are worth one point! What else can I do?" Lucy grumped.

"That's when you use other people's words," said Gran, starting a word by adding an "s" to "axe" on a triple-word score, then using up all the rest of her tiles and making a ridiculously huge number of points.

"I feel sick," Alicia said.

"I don't blame you — that's a tricky hand," said Gran, peeking at Alicia's letters. "But even so, in this family, *honour* is spelled with a *u*."

"But *honor* is correct!" Alicia said. "And don't look at my letters!"

"Correct, incorrect — I don't care," Gran said. "We're playing Canadian spelling."

"My teacher said Canadians spell it both ways," Becca said.

"Not these Canadians," said Gran. "Alicia, you're looking green around the gills. You shouldn't take it so seriously. A bad hand is just something that happens sometimes. It's all about what you do with —"

"I don't ..." said Alicia, sounding more uncertain than Becca had ever heard her. "Gran, I ..."

And suddenly Alicia was off and running, blundering into the cabin with a great crashing of doors and thunder of footfalls.

"Well!" said Gran. "What's that about, I wonder? It's not like her to be so sensitive."

"It can't really be about spelling," Becca said. "Can it?"

"If she cares that much about spelling she must take after me," said Gran, looking pleased. "Better go see what her problem is, Becca. We don't want the game to go on forever."

But the sounds Becca heard coming from the bathroom were not about spelling.

Unless, of course, Alicia had had alphabet soup for lunch.

And even Uncle Martin at the worst of his seasickness had not sounded as nasty as Alicia did now.

"She's sick," Becca reported back to Gran.

"The chicken salad," Lucy said. "I knew we shouldn't eat it."

"Well, there's not much we can do for her if she had bad food," Gran said. "It's a suitable start to the summer visit — out with the old. Your turn now, Lucy."

Becca went back to Alicia.

"They're still playing Scrabble," she told her.

"I feel horrible," said Alicia. "I'm never eating chicken salad again." And with a shudder, she bent over the toilet.

It really was disgusting. Becca reached over and flushed.

"Becca! Becca! Bring me a bag!" shouted Gran. "A basin! A bucket!"

Becca hurried to the back door and snatched up a bucket. She ran back to the beach.

"Just in time!" Gran said.

Lucy clutched her stomach and groaned. Becca didn't wait to see what happened. Anyway, she could hear all too well. The evening had become full of awful sound effects.

She ran back to Alicia.

"I can't stop," Alicia moaned. "It just keeps coming and coming!"

"Do you want a wet cloth for your face?" Becca asked.

Mum did that sometimes when Becca was sick. Becca started to run water in the sink.

The water ran, Alicia exploded again, and an alarm went off in the house — a great clanging and buzzing that filled the air. An ear-tearing, nose-wateringly high scream that made Becca think the firefighters would show up.

Where were Merlin and Mrs. Barker and all the rest of them with their hoses and fire extinguishers? Why would throwing up cause a fire alarm? And where was Aunt Fifi when she needed her?

Lucy's eruptions sounded in the distance, and now Gran was bellowing from the beach again.

On and on it went — a clamor that filled the bathroom and Becca's ears and Alicia's, too.

It was coming from under the sink.

"Oh, for crying in the sink!" moaned Alicia. "Oh, save me!" And once more she bent to the toilet. Tears streamed down her face.

Heave away, Johnny, Becca thought. She banged open the cupboard under the sink. Rubber gloves with holes in, empty shampoo bottles, soap as hard as stone. Why did Gran keep all this rubbish? Becca couldn't see a thing there that would make such a noise.

"Gran!" she shouted.

She ran back to the beach.

Gran was holding the bucket for Lucy in one hand, and holding Lucy's hair back with the other.

"What? It must be the sewage system alarm," Gran said, looking alarmed herself. "Why would that happen? Plumbing! And Fifi's here! It never fails. What, again, Lucy? Will this never end?"

No wonder Gran was so picky about her plumbing. But who would expect two sick-to-their-stomach people and a sewage alarm, all at the same time?

* * *

After a thousand trips back and forth, and the worst kind of familiarity with Alicia's chicken salad, and a clamorous hour with Gran's sewage system alarm (if that's what it was), and a long episode of Gran showing Becca how a fuse box worked, and the successful tying up of several stinking bags of stuff now ready for the laundromat, and the swilling of several disgusting buckets in the sea ("The crabs will enjoy it," said Gran) — Becca and Gran sat together again on the twilit beach. Alicia and Lucy were all washed up and put to bed on the back deck — outdoors, said Gran, which would make everything easier if their unfortunate condition recurred.

"Did you call Merlin?" Becca asked.

"I left a message on his machine," said Gran. "He's out. Of course! Thank goodness I found the fuse to turn the alarm off, but we're going to have to use the biffy until he gives us a diagnosis."

Merlin! Becca could ask him if he had a copy of *The Tempest.*

"It feels like Lucy and Alicia have been here for a very long time," said Gran. "Is it really possible that they arrived only a couple of hours ago? Now, let's get back to this Scrabble board. I'll just set the lantern here so we can see, and you can play Alicia's hand and I'll play Lucy's. Ew!" she added cheerfully, taking over Lucy's letters. "What a terrible hand!"

It was going to be a long night.

4. Waterworks

~~~~~~

In the morning Merlin was there, limping but mobile.

"It was a mild sprain," he said. "Before you ask. And I don't know what the problem is," he went on, checking out the pipes and pumps of Gran's water arrangements. "Everything here looks as usual, which is to say strange but functional. Fifi! What remarkable sleepwear."

"I didn't realize we'd be entertaining so early in the morning." Aunt Fifi yawned, stalking out of the house in the world's oldest bathing suit. "At least I'm wearing more than I was last time you came for breakfast."

Becca remembered the morning Merlin had arrived in his fire-chief outfit to put out a chimney fire, and Aunt Fifi had appeared in nothing but a small towel.

Merlin smiled and turned to Gran. "The alarm might be for some other part of the system," he said, and started off into a long speech that involved words like "septic field," "discharge pump" and "thousands of dollars."

Gran looked more and more depressed.

Then Merlin went off and hung his head down in the manhole for the watery part of the sewage system and mumbled about this and that, while Gran yelled up from the house that the alarm was still buzzing and Becca relayed their messages.

"It could be electrical," Merlin said, his head emerging at last. "That's not my job. You'd better disconnect the fuse again. I can't seem to do anything to stop it doing its alarm thing from in here."

"You might as well stay for coffee, now that you're here," said Aunt Fifi. "And have some breakfast."

"Not a good idea," Gran said, but she put the kettle on. And Aunt Fifi made conversation in quite a civilized way.

"Somebody's been out fishing very early," she said. "There's a nice runabout pulled up on the sand down there."

Becca told Merlin about putting on a play to raise funds for a better boat.

"Of course, Lucy and Alicia are going to have to want to be part owners of a sailboat," she said. "But maybe they'll do it because it'll be fun."

"I do have some copies of *The Tempest*," Merlin said. "You're welcome to them."

"Jane and I and Lucy and Alicia will be the actors," Becca said. "I hope."

"Four people should be just enough," said Merlin.

"The tide's about to turn," said Gran. "That fellow had better retrieve his boat before it's awash."

Merlin had toast and one of Kay-next-door's double-yolked eggs with the bright-orange yolks. He was just like one of the family.

"What excellent marmalade," he commented. "Homemade!"

"Most of it was scraped off Lucy's clothes," Becca told him.

"Sounds like family politics," he said. "Fifi! Can we take our coffee out onto the deck? Are you having anything to do with this production of *The Tempest*?"

"No talking about Shakespeare!" Gran said now. "I forbid it!"

Merlin used to be a Shakespeare actor, and now he was a plumber. He still knew lots about plays, though.

And so did Aunt Fifi. She taught Shakespeare at a university. Last summer, she and Merlin had argued a lot. Becca had seen that they liked arguing, and that they even liked each other.

But Gran was always afraid. What if Aunt Fifi made Merlin seriously furious? Would he stomp off forever, leaving Gran without his vital services?

Aunt Fifi and Merlin were already out on the deck with their coffee.

"Of course I'll help out," Aunt Fifi declared.

Becca looked out at the bay. She was feeling like she had lived through exactly this moment before. She remembered the time Aunt Fifi and Merlin had stayed up all night, looking after Merlin's runaway boat and arguing. Now, out in the bay, she could see the little runabout that had been pulled up on the sand, and it wasn't pulled up on the sand anymore.

It was floating free, unmoored and unmanned.

"The wind's blowing out of the bay, right?" she asked. "Winds from the southeast, fifteen to twenty knots?"

That's what Dugald had said.

"If Fifi's helping I'll help, too," Merlin said to her. "You can't let literary types loose with live theater. You need someone who knows about the practical side of it."

Did they even want Merlin and Aunt Fifi messed up in this play? Becca wondered. But out loud she said, "That boat's drifting out to sea."

The little boat was quite far out now, bobbing up and down in the chop whipped up by the cheerful southeasterly breeze. It was heading northwest at a steady pace. It wasn't in danger of capsizing, but its owner was going to be stranded when he or she came back and wanted to go home. And then there would be the bother of trying to find the boat, floating around in the middle of the strait somewhere. Or someone might claim it as salvage, and the owner might never get it back.

How would Becca feel if that was *Gull*? Or worse, the new, glorious boat they would acquire, eventually, she hoped?

"I have no idea who owns it," Gran said.

"We should rescue it," said Becca.

"Yes," said Gran. "Come along, Becca. It's a hazard to leave Fifi and Merlin together, but someone has to bring in that boat."

And before Becca could ask any questions, she found herself hauling *Glaucous Gull* down the beach with Gran, all loaded up with oars and life jackets.

Becca heard a faint cry from the deck.

"They think we should take the motor," said Gran.

Becca thought about the motor still stowed away for the winter, locked up in the shed next to a fuel tank with an unknown amount of old fuel in it.

"It would take too long," she said.

"Heave!" Gran instructed.

They lifted *Gull* over the last rocks and onto the sand.

"Push!" said Gran, shoving *Gull* into the sea. Even before the water was up to Becca's knees, Gran had hopped into *Gull* and was fitting the oarlocks in place.

"Jump in," she said. "You take one oar and I'll take the other."

Becca sat next to her and seized the oar.

"You have to row in time with me," said Gran.

Becca tried, but *Gull* kept drifting broadside to the waves.

"Pull!" said Gran.

Becca got a grip on her oar. She pulled short choppy strokes, and Gran rowed with long powerful ones.

The wind wasn't strong, but it was steady. The runaway boat bounced in the waves, tipping this way then that, heading out beyond the point.

But *Gull* was having trouble getting out of the shallows. Becca kept struggling to stroke together with Gran.

Or perhaps it was Gran who wasn't managing, Becca thought, as Gran dug her oar so deep that it hit the sand at the bottom of the bay.

Sometimes the waves tilted one side of *Gull* towards the water, and sometimes the other. Sometimes Becca's oar was in the water, and sometimes she was pulling on air. Sometimes she had her feet braced on the boat, and sometimes the waves tried to tip her right off the thwart.

"Pull, Becca!" Gran cried.

And as she shouted, Gran pulled deeply, mightily with both of her considerably muscular arms. She pulled once, twice, three times, just as Becca's oar lifted right out of the sea.

There was an enormous cracking bang.

Becca slid towards Gran, but Gran herself was tipping, lurching, falling — and then Becca was, too.

She felt *Gull* toss her off, and the cold sea closed over her head. It sucked right up into her nose and her gasping mouth.

Capsized!

She didn't want to drown! she thought. She wanted to live! And to have adventures with Jane, and put on a play, and get a nice boat that wouldn't throw her into the sea!

She flailed her arms and legs, and her shorts and her shirt dragged and tugged, and her head was full of sea — all the way through to her ears! — and the ocean blurred in her eyes, and seaweed caught at her hands. She could feel her sweater float wetly right up into her face.

Then she felt her knees on the sand below and she pushed her head out of the water.

"Greetings," said Gran.

Her face streamed with sea and her own hair.

Becca saw that they were under *Gull*. Gran's head and shoulders poked up out of the water and into the air trapped by *Gull*'s hull, and Becca's did, too. Gran's voice clanged as it echoed in the aluminum hull.

It was like they were in a little cabin of air surrounded by sea.

Becca could breathe.

And the water was shallow, only up to her neck.

She coughed bitter sea.

"Will you look at that crab," said Gran, staring down into the water. "It's huge. We should grab it for dinner."

Aunt Fifi and Merlin appeared suddenly, hauling *Gull* up by the gunwales.

"What are you doing under there, Mum?" Aunt Fifi asked.

Aunt Fifi and Merlin had waded right into the sea, and Merlin's jeans billowed in the waves. The two of them didn't seem to care that they were getting sodden.

"Are you all right, Becca?" Aunt Fifi asked.

"What happened, Isobel?" Merlin asked, holding *Gull* so Becca and Gran could clamber out from underneath.

"I really don't know," said Gran, sitting in water up to her neck.

Becca waded out through the waves, where one of *Gull*'s oars bobbed up and down. The oarlock had broken, she saw. Snapped off completely.

No wonder they'd heard a bang.

Well, that was that. Could there be a clearer sign that they needed another boat? She looked up and there was the runaway boat tossing in the southeasterly swell, now officially out of the bay and at sea.

Up on the rocks, Bill-and-Kay-next-door were dragging their own boat down to the water. It had its motor on and its own boat wheels, and they had launched it and Bill was off over the waves to haul in the runaway in only a few minutes. And here came a couple of neighbors, too, from over the bay, drawn from their breakfasts by the drama.

"Quite a show," said Merlin as he and Aunt Fifi strode out of the sea carrying *Gull*. "What were you doing? Rehearsing *The Tempest*'s shipwreck?"

"No talking about Shakespeare!" said Gran. "Look! I nabbed a crab for dinner. A Dungeness!"

"Better not be too bossy," said Aunt Fifi. "He's the only plumber on the island. And by the way, is that crab legal? It looks kind of small to me."

Then she and Merlin laughed as they carried *Gull* over the sandstone and up onto the driftwood.

"Well, that was amusing," Gran commented after they'd changed their clothes, and Merlin had changed into Grandpa's old mustard-colored sweater and elastic-less sweatpants.

"What a production," said Aunt Fifi.

"Speaking of which, I'll leave *The Tempest* for you in the free post at the store," Merlin told Becca. "And don't worry. You're off to a great start with the opening scene."

Then he rushed off to his next appointment.

"Why are those clothes all soaked?" asked Lucy, wandering out in her pajamas.

"All the interesting stuff happens when I'm away or asleep," complained Alicia.

"You should get up earlier," said Becca. She stood on the chopping block to peg the sea-sodden clothes to the clothesline.

"Goodness, now we have Merlin's laundry," Aunt Fifi said, and then she marched off to the well to get water, as if it was a perfectly normal day of chores. "What next?"

5. The Tide Came In and Took It

~~~~~~

"Now *Gull* isn't just slow. She has a broken oarlock, too,"
Becca said.

"Never mind," said Jane. "We're going to do this play
and earn money and then, after tons and tons of chores and
saving our allowance for years, we'll have a boat with two
completely non-broken oarlocks that we never use because
it sails perfectly."

"Gannet," said Becca.

"What?" Jane asked. "Look — Dad had to get stuff from
the store so I went with him and picked up Merlin's copies
of the play. Let's read it through and see how it goes. That's
what we did at school."

"We could name it *Gannet*," Becca explained. "It's a bird
that never has to come to land. Basically."

Jane pushed a copy of *The Tempest* into Becca's hand.

"Whoa," Becca said. "We might need help with this."

"It's not so bad," said Jane. "If you read it fast and don't
bother trying to figure out what all the words mean, you can
understand it pretty well."

They sat on Mermaid's Rock. Then they lay on it. First

they lay on their stomachs and read, and when they got to Act Three, they lay on their backs and read.

Then they sat up again for Acts Four and Five.

Some bits were hard to understand and some bits weren't. Jane was right.

The story had three kinds of people — romantic ones and mopey ones and funny ones. There was a magician, two sweethearts and a sprite named Ariel, and a group of shipwrecked noblemen who sat around a lot, and a monster-fish-man named Caliban, and a couple of clowns who sang, danced, stole laundry and tried to take over the island.

It took ages to read it out loud. The sea, which started out way far away in the regions of sand dollars and eelgrass, crept up as they read until it was licking at the barnacles on Mermaid's Rock.

At last Jane said the magician Prospero's final speech. She stood up and spoke out over the rocks, as if the gulls and oystercatchers were her audience.

"'What strength I have's mine own, which is most faint ...'" she declared. Then she added, "I do feel faint. I'm starved."

Becca felt as though she'd been far, far away, blundering in swamps and forests, flying over a stormy sea and making thunderous magic with the characters in the story. For a while she'd forgotten everything — Lucy, Alicia, the tide, her very self.

"Let's go to my place for lunch," said Jane. "Dad got some excellent food. Luckily he's open to taking advice when shopping."

"I have to tell Gran or one of the aunts," said Becca, coming back into the world. "I'll be back in a minute."

*   *   *

Becca heard a car door slam and the murmur of voices up in the driveway.

Auntie Meg!

Everything about *The Tempest* went out of her head. She thought of *Betsy had a baby* ... and *the tide came in and took it and 'twas never seen no more.*

Last summer, Auntie Meg had been pregnant. Becca had been the only cousin who noticed then, but during the winter, when Auntie Meg was back on the little island where she and Uncle Martin lived, she got bigger and bigger. She sent pictures.

But then something happened. Somehow, it all went wrong. The baby wasn't alive any more, even though she was almost ready to be born.

Nobody knew why the baby didn't live. Mum and Dad, Becca and Pin sent a hazelnut tree to plant in her memory.

Becca had talked about it with Mum and Dad, and with Gran, and she had talked to Auntie Meg and Uncle Martin on the phone.

There should be a baby out in the world now, a new cousin who was Auntie Meg and Uncle Martin's family. And there wasn't.

What had that been like for Auntie Meg? And even though it had happened months ago, what was it like for her now, empty-armed? That's what Uncle Martin called it when he talked to Becca on the phone at that sad time.

Becca hadn't seen Auntie Meg since then.

Her feet slowed on the path as she thought about the cousin she would never know.

Then she could see them, Auntie Meg and Gran, hugging and hugging.

Becca couldn't help it. She threw her arms around them.

"Dearest Becca," said Auntie Meg.

Auntie Meg was the aunt who was always full of love.

Becca looked up at her. She had never seen Auntie Meg unable to smile before.

"Auntie Meg," Becca said, and she squeezed and squeezed, and hugged every part of Auntie Meg and Gran she could reach.

"Oh, Becca!" Gran said.

For a moment she looked about two hundred years old. Becca actually felt her tremble.

Gran, trembling! And with tears in her eyes.

Then Gran shook her head, shook the drops from her eyes, and seemed to shake herself all over.

"Well," she said, and picked up Auntie Meg's bag.

Auntie Meg's face gathered itself together as Becca watched, and she turned to get the rest of her luggage out of the car.

*　*　*

DEIRDRE BAKER

Becca ran back to Jane. She tried very hard to think about the play.

"Alicia," she said. "Alicia'd be a perfect Prospero. He's always bossing people around and making things work out the way he wants. And you were so good at barking and growling at the otters. You could be Caliban, the monster-fish-man. You can roll in the otters' bedroom to get the right smell. And we'll get something fish-scaly for you to wear."

"Gee, thanks," said Jane.

They jumped across slippery sea lettuce.

"Would Lucy be a good Miranda?" Jane asked.

"Will she be good at falling in love? Miranda has to fall in love."

But Becca's mind was really still full of Auntie Meg. Sea-sorrow. That was a word from Shakespeare's play and that's what the play was about, partly. Shipwreck and losing things, especially daughters and sons.

Prospero and Shakespeare made things come out all right.

But nothing could make things come right for Auntie Meg and Uncle Martin and their baby-to-be.

Think about *The Tempest*, she told herself. Or think about sailing a ship called *Gannet*, or *Pigeon Guillemot*, or even *Sea Otter* — all seafaring creatures.

"Look at the eagle," Jane said, stopping suddenly.

High, squeaking calls cascaded down from the eaglet in the nest near Jane's cabin. And out over the sea flashed the bright head and tail of an adult eagle looking for lunch, making big airy flaps as it patrolled the strait.

"There isn't so much salmon now," Jane said. "Uncle Mac said."

The eagle swooped in a big curve and flew back the way it had come.

"The eagles are hungry. Merlin said he saw one trying to carry off someone's little poodle!"

"Mum says she remembers when her dad and Uncle Mac brought in buckets and buckets of fish, day after day," said Jane.

The eagle was turning again. Becca looked up at its white head shining in the sunlight. It flew over her, low enough that she could hear the beating of its wings on the air, the low, forceful noise of sky being pushed.

Whoosh! There it went, plunging and then leveling out, raking its feet through the water and dragging a salmon in a flurry of splashes beneath it.

"Look! It caught something!" Jane said.

"Something huge!"

"Lift!" Jane shouted.

"Heave away, eagle, all bound to go," Becca called out.

The eagle pumped its wings, but it still wasn't much above the water.

"That must be some heavy fish," said Jane.

"Look — it's going to row. Or swim, sort of."

The eagle was pulling its wings through the water as if it was doing the butterfly stroke.

"I didn't know eagles could swim," Jane said.

"Why is it trying to swim? Why doesn't it fly?"

It couldn't, Becca suddenly realized. It couldn't get liftoff with the heavy salmon in its talons.

She ran with Jane down to the tide's edge, where the sandstone shelves dropped off down to the subtidal homes of sea urchins, sea cucumbers and kelp beds, and then down beyond that to the realms of rockfish, wolf eels and gobies.

The eagle pulled its wings through the water again and again. Becca thought she could almost hear it panting, it was working so hard. It made her breathe hard herself, trying to lend the strength of her own breath so it could get up, up out of the sea and into the sky where it should be.

"It's slowing down," Jane said. "What's it going to do?"

The splash of the eagle's rowing mingled with the splash of the fish that was under water, clutched in its talons.

"It's a big salmon," said Becca.

"If we had a boat we could help it," said Jane, but Becca didn't think so. She didn't think an eagle would let itself be helped that way.

"Why doesn't it just let go of the fish?"

"Maybe it's stubborn," said Jane.

"Maybe it can't." Becca realized that she was clasping her hands, squeezing her fingers as if her own wishing could give the eagle strength.

But the eagle's wings moved slowly and heavily now. It could hardly lift them out of the water.

"You can do it. You can do it. You can do it," she muttered. She hardly noticed that her feet were soggy, that she and Jane were standing right in the sea, as if they were trying to get as close to the eagle as they could.

{54}

The eagle slogged and strained.

Everything seemed to happen slowly then. The eagle gave an exhausted push with its wings.

"Oh!" said Jane.

Quietly, slowly, the eagle disappeared beneath the sea.

Before Becca's and Jane's surprised eyes the water burbled. Bubbles floated on the surface for a minute, and then it was as if that eagle and salmon had never been.

Right before their eyes, but hidden from them, underwater, the eagle was sinking. There wasn't a thing they could do about it.

The tide came in and took it and 'twas never seen no more, Becca thought.

"It isn't fair!" Jane said. "What if it's the mum or dad of the eaglet in the nest by our cabin?"

"But the fish might live," Becca said. "Instead of being eaten by the eagle."

"But how could it, if the eagle is still hooked into it?" asked Jane. "It isn't fair."

"Nature isn't fair or unfair," Becca said. "That's what Gran would say. It just is."

And, she thought, Auntie Meg's baby dying wasn't fair or not fair. It just was.

But that didn't make it not sad.

She had to stop still for a minute, waiting for her face to go into its proper shape again, and her eyes to stop being blurry.

Jane looked out to where the eagle had sunk out of sight.

Becca looked at the sea, too.

"After the eagle's dead it will feed other sea creatures," she said. "I mean, they'll eat every bit of it so it will be giving life in a way. And they'll eat the salmon, too, just the way the eagle would have."

"I know. But it's still horrible."

"*The Tempest* has sea-sorrow in it," Becca said.

"Yes, they get sad when they think the prince has drowned," said Jane. "But he doesn't really drown. Not like this eagle. Or fish."

"It's a story about a magician who tries to make things fair," said Becca.

They couldn't make things fair, not for the eagle or for Auntie Meg and Uncle Martin. But Becca thought about how the play had taken her away for a time, the way a good story could do.

Maybe a play could do that for Auntie Meg. It might give her heart a rest.

Even if it was only for a little while.

6. Flying

~~~~~~

Auntie Meg put her arms around Becca.

"Of course I'm sad," she said.

She was quite still then, and Becca hugged her and smelled her good Auntie Meg smell, a mixture of flowery soap, bicycle grease and Douglas fir.

"You would have been an excellent mum," Becca said. "You're such a good rower and sailor."

"We still hope I'll be a mum some day," Auntie Meg said. "And to practice, maybe you and I could go rowing or sailing together."

"Or probably both," Becca said. "Because of how *Gull* is."

She and Auntie Meg were in the community garden, but even so they could hear the eagle parents near Jane's cabin having their high, hoarse conversations — and the eaglet, too, with a quick series of notes that were like a squeaking laugh.

So that eaglet still had its mum and dad.

Becca picked kale leaves, and then she pinched off some of the yellow flowers to put in the salad.

Auntie Meg cut some sprigs of mint and rosemary. Becca pulled up a few tiny carrots so the others would have more room to grow.

Nobody else was in the garden. The sweetpeas were covered with their first flowers — pink and white and purple and blue — each breathing its scent into the air. The frothy baby's breath and summer roses of Kay-next-door's garden swayed in the wind.

* * *

"Gran said the eagle couldn't retract its talons," Becca told Jane. "She said they were probably stuck far into the fish and when the fish turned out to be so heavy, it was fatal."

"I'm glad it wasn't one of our baby eagle's parents," said Jane. "They're still here, and the eaglet's screeching away like stink."

"And then Gran rushed away to tell Merlin's brother-in-law Arnulf where to dump the load of wood he delivered," Becca continued. "But before she went she said nature isn't right or wrong. It just is."

"She sounds like you," Jane said. "Or you sound like her."

* * *

"So, what do I have to do for this?" Lucy asked.

"We're just going to read our parts right now," said Becca. "Even though Alicia isn't here yet."

"Yet? She said no," said Lucy. "She said, quote, I'm too

old to play with you kids. Plus, Shakespeare's for school. End quote."

They were sitting in the treehouse at Jane's, near the otters' bedroom but high in the trees.

Above them was Jane's cabin, and the tree that was the home of a bald eagle family. From the treehouse Becca could see the mattress of sticks that was their nest near the top of a Douglas fir.

And she could hear them, just like Jane said. *Screech, screech, screech* went the baby eagle, nonstop.

Really, being in the treehouse was like being in an eagle's nest. A perfect *Tempest* place, airy but surrounded by sea.

"Oh, man, I don't know if I'm ever going to understand this," Lucy said, staring at her book. "Plus, there's no way I'll remember it."

"Just try," Becca said.

"What are those eagles screeching about?" Lucy asked.

"They're yelling at the baby," said Jane. "They start early in the morning and pretty much go on until dark. I think they want it to fly."

A clashing clamor arose from the trees. It made Becca think of *The Tempest*, and how the island was full of noises, like "a thousand twangling instruments that clang about the ears."

"They're so loud!" she said.

"It's just the baby eagle," said Jane. "Well, he's not really a baby now. More like a kid."

Becca tried to get everyone going with the play, but the eagle family's discussion suddenly rose to an enormous ruckus. Lucy forgot to read her part.

"What!" she said.

"It's eagles! It's normal!" Jane said. "You get used to it. Well, sort of."

"It sounds like fighting," Lucy complained. "I hate fighting."

"It's not a fight," Jane said. "It's an eaglet growing up."

Up against the blue, on the top of the tree, the eagle mother stared down her beak into the nest.

"See, there," said Jane. "You can see its head."

Screech, screech, went the mother. The sound was like fingernails on a blackboard. Lucy put her hands over her ears.

Now Becca could see the eaglet, all scruffy and brown. It stepped up near the edge of the nest and flapped its wings.

"It's doing exercises," she said.

The mother flew to a nearby tree and glared back at it.

"She's trying to teach it, I bet," said Jane.

But apparently the eaglet didn't want to learn to fly. It disappeared back into the nest, and the mother eagle dropped into the nest, too.

"Okay," Becca said. "Back to the play."

In the play, Prospero was bossing his slave, the sprite Ariel. Lucy acted Ariel, and she was not too bad at it.

"I've had lots of experience being bossed around," she said.

When they finished that scene, she went back to gazing at the eagles.

"The baby's looking over the edge again," she reported.

But now Jane was growling and snorting as Caliban the monster-fish-man. Becca couldn't really pay attention to Lucy and the eaglet. In her Caliban voice Jane sounded a bit like the otters, as if she was crunching on fishbones hard as crockery. You had to really pay attention to understand her, never mind to understand Shakespeare's funny way of talking.

"'A south-west wind blow on ye and blister you all o'er!'" Jane ranted, and then she and Lucy went on to be the lovers, Miranda and Ferdinand.

The play raced along.

"More enthusiasm!" cried Becca.

"What?" Lucy asked, but at that moment the eagles roused themselves to such a pitch of clangorous twitterings that Becca could hardly hear her.

The eaglet was on eagle-tiptoe on the edge of the nest. It flapped its wings up and down, up and down, as if it was flexing its muscles.

"It's teetering," said Jane.

The mother loomed over it.

"It's going to fly!" Lucy said. "It's going to give it a go!"

With a blur of flapping, the eaglet hopped off the nest, out into the air.

Becca didn't know an airborne bird could wobble so much. The eaglet lurched in the sky, flapping desperately and crying out with alarm. It didn't seem at all sure about flying.

It came to a crashing sort of landing on a nearby branch.

"All that noise," said Lucy. "It didn't get very far."

"It was its first time," Becca said.

"They usually go farther than that," Jane said. "Last year the baby eagles from this nest really cruised around."

But this eaglet just hunched on its branch.

"Its eyes are squinched shut," Lucy said.

"You can't really see that," said Jane.

"No, but if it was me my eyes would be squinched shut," said Lucy.

The eaglet's wings were furled tight around it. It turned its head aside, away from its mother.

"No way is it going to fly back," said Lucy.

"But it can't sleep there," Becca said. "It will fall off!"

"Don't eagles sleep standing up?" Jane asked. "Anyway, it's ages 'til bedtime."

The eaglet actually seemed to be quivering with fear.

"It'll go eventually," Becca said at last. "Whoever heard of an eaglet who was chicken?"

Maybe it just wasn't grown enough, like a little kid too small to ride a bike.

"I want to see what happens," said Lucy.

"But we have to practice!" Becca said. "We can't watch birds all day. And you guys should sound more enthusiastic about the romance stuff. You're supposed to be all lovey-dovey, so don't look bored! Miranda shouldn't call Ferdinand "a thing divine" and sound like she's, I don't know, searching under the sink for toilet cleaner."

"I never would," said Lucy. "I hate cleaning toilets."

Up in the fir tree, the eaglet cowered as if its feet were stuck to the branch, as if its talons were actually growing into the tree's flesh.

And it looked like it had pushed its beak right into the tree trunk, like it was anchored at both ends.

Down in the treehouse, Jane went into her Caliban-the-monster-fish-man mode again and Becca and Lucy read the parts of the two clowns and sang and danced.

And then they did the scene where the shipwrecked noblemen sat around moping — the people the magician was getting revenge on.

"Not revenge, exactly," said Jane.

"He's just trying to make things fair again, because they stole his country and pushed him out to sea without any oars," Becca said.

"Just like us!" said Jane.

Overhead, nothing changed. The eaglet sat and the mother nattered at it. Sometimes she flew back and forth.

The tide turned and the sun reached them from a different part of the sky.

The whole time the eaglet and its mum talked, or maybe argued. Every once in a while the mum coaxed the eaglet to move a little way out on the branch.

The mum would fly by, as if she was showing the eaglet what to do.

Then the eaglet would look down, and that was that. It shuffled back towards the trunk of the tree.

"That's some stubborn bird," said Lucy.

"It's scared," Becca said.

"It must be hungry by now," Jane said. "Usually it eats, eats, eats all day."

The eaglet squawked and the mum answered with her high twittering squeaks.

In the play, Miranda and Ferdinand got married.

Then Caliban and the clowns got lost in a swamp.

"'We are such stuff as dreams are made on,'" Becca said in the voice of Prospero the magician, and for a minute it was like they were in a different world up in the treehouse, perched between land and sea, earth and sky, and with eagles having family time nearby.

"I'm ready for a swim," said Jane.

"Oh, let's just get through the last act," Becca said. "It won't take long."

She really felt like the magician in the play, suddenly. He was always worrying about running out of time.

The mother eagle flew towards them from across Midshipman Bay, and just as Becca was gathering herself for the very last words of the play, she felt a drip.

"It can't be raining," she said.

But drips were definitely falling.

And the mother eagle had just flown right over them.

"Ew!" said Lucy. "What's she holding?"

"It's a fish," Becca said. "It's a dead fish with its guts hanging out. Dripping! Look!"

She pointed to her arm, wet with drips of pink fish juice.

"She's flying past the eaglet," Jane said. "She's tempting it back to the nest."

"With juicy innards!" said Lucy. "Yum!"

Mother and eaglet called to each other.

The eaglet reached out and opened and shut its beak.

"Look!" Becca said. "It's trying to grab it."

The mother eagle came to rest on the edge of the nest, the fish clutched in her talons.

The eaglet began to work its wings, complaining.

"I've never seen this before," said Jane. "Other times our eagles didn't act like this."

"It's going to go," Lucy said, speaking very quietly.

Becca found herself holding her breath. The eaglet tottered on the edge of its branch.

The mother eagle dangled the fish. It was as if she was using willpower to get her eaglet home. Pulling it with its hunger for fish and fish guts.

The eaglet opened its wings.

It jumped up towards the nest.

It worked its wings madly, and its jump was almost like flight.

It was a big jump and it seemed to take a really long time.

Holding her breath, Becca started to get that feeling of strangeness that would mean she'd have to let it go. But she didn't want to. She felt somehow that if the eaglet couldn't make it to the nest in the space of a girl's breath, it wasn't going to get there at all. It would fall — crash down through the branches and end up broken. Or dead, even.

"It's going to make it," Lucy muttered. "I know it will. I know it will."

Time seemed to stop. The eaglet flapped, the mother waved the dripping fish, the breeze blew the swagging branches of the Douglas firs.

With one last effortful pump of its wings, the eaglet scrabbled over the edge of the nest, tumbled into it and disappeared.

With great gusts everyone breathed out, and in again — a windy chorus that could have carried the eaglet home with its warm force.

"It worked!" Lucy said. "I knew it would."

But Becca met Jane's eyes.

They hadn't been sure, thinking of the other eagle and fish they had seen.

There wasn't any rule to make it have a good ending. It wasn't like one of Shakespeare's happy plays where you knew everything would come out all right at the end.

It was a sort of luck, Becca thought. You didn't know.

Sometimes things worked out all right, and sometimes they didn't.

7. The Clothesline

~~~~~~

"But what if I don't want to be in a play?" Alicia said. "It sounds like a ton of work. All those lines. It would take eighty million hours to memorize it. And even then we couldn't understand it."

Alicia's stomach was fine now but she insisted on lying about, all pale and weak-looking. Becca thought it was an act. And if she was going to act, she might as well be in the play.

"We can understand it," Becca said. "Mostly."

"Acting's better than pulling couch grass or washing the toilet," said Lucy. "Which is what Gran will get you to do if you aren't doing something else."

Lucy was nursing blisters from her morning chores. But it was her own fault for using a trowel to turn the compost instead of the shovel, which was way more efficient.

"I don't want a boat anyway," Alicia went on. "Sailing is boring. I want a motor scooter — one of those Italian ones."

"I guess we could do it without you," Becca said. "But …"

"It'll be fun," said Jane. "You know it will."

"And Lucy's right. It might get you out of some chores," Becca said. "Gran said before Auntie Clare arrives she wants

{67}

to clean out the tool shed and the loft. You know what that means. And the play's for a good cause."

"You really are dreaming if you think it will get you out of some chores," said Alicia. "And I don't think you wanting a boat is especially a good cause. What Auntie Clare and Uncle Clarence do is a good cause, working with orphans and grandmothers and sick people in Africa." She turned over on her towel so she was facing away from them. "You just want to have fun."

"What's wrong with fun?" asked Jane.

Alicia flapped her hand at them.

Becca thought about the play. Some of what Alicia said was true. It was too long, at least for the sort of show she and Jane and Lucy could put on. They would have to cut out a lot of lines, and maybe some characters, too.

"We've got Lucy," said Jane. "And if Alicia won't do it, I can play Prospero. Probably. And we can switch roles around some more."

"But you're so excellent as Caliban the monster-fish-man," Becca said.

"We could figure out a way for me to do both," said Jane. "I'm just saying. If we need to."

But Becca was sure Alicia had to be Prospero — forceful as she was. A bit like an Aunt Fifi in the making. Or even Gran!

They just had to find a way to make her want to do it.

"We'll figure it out," she said. "Anyway, for now there are some words we don't get, and some that are weird but make sense if you think about them, like 'o'erstunk' and 'up-staring.'"

"I like 'o'erstunk,'" said Jane. "It suits a person who lives by an otter family's bedroom."

"The main thing is that some characters just go on and on. And lots of times their jokes are barely funny," said Becca.

"They might be funny if we knew what they meant," said Jane.

"Let's just keep the jokes we like," said Becca.

"And the lines we like the sound of," said Jane. "Like 'hedgehogs tumbling in my barefoot way.' Even if we don't know exactly what they mean."

"We can ask Aunt Fifi to help us shorten it and keep it sensible," Becca said.

"Or Merlin," said Jane.

"But not both," said Becca, thinking of Gran and her efforts to keep Merlin and Aunt Fifi away from Shakespeare.

* * *

"Of course I'll help," said Aunt Fifi. "What do you want me to do?"

She was on a wood-chopping rampage. Bit by bit, she was chopping up the logs in the woodshed, making way for the wood Merlin's brother-in-law had dumped for Gran.

Becca stood a little distance away, but she could feel the brisk puff of air each time Aunt Fifi brought the axe down.

"This alder is perfect for splitting," Aunt Fifi said, and with a blow the alder log fell into two beautiful chunks.

"Fifi! You should take the laundry down first," said Gran. "Those are Merlin's things waving about over the woodpile."

"Well, he should stop by and collect them," said Aunt Fifi in three gusty breaths as she whacked at the alder. "They've been hanging here for days. And I'm busy. Does he really need to air his underpants at our house?"

"Take it easy," Gran said. "He's a busy man. He's the only plumber on the island! And leave some of that wood in big pieces so it will hold the fire when I use it in winter."

"Aye, aye, sir," said Aunt Fifi, attacking another log.

The clothesline ran right near the woodpile. Becca wanted to hang up her bathing suit, but with Aunt Fifi swinging the axe around so fast it felt dangerous. She got up on Gran's stoop and pulled in the line so she could pin her things next to Merlin's still-damp shirt and jeans and underwear. That way she didn't have to go so close to Aunt Fifi.

Whack! Aunt Fifi swung the axe again. All the exertion was making her pink in the face.

"We *are* going to need your help with the play," Becca told her. "We need to make it shorter and cut out bits that are hard to understand."

"Any time," said Aunt Fifi, punctuating her offer with a sharp blow. "As long as Merlin isn't sticking his nose in, too. He has outlandish notions about Shakespeare. He thinks Prospero is nothing but a blowhard!"

She bent for another log. Becca's bathing suit and Merlin's damp clothes bounced as Becca moved them along, and the pulleys at either end of the line screeched like excited gulls.

"Most people cut lines when they do Shakespeare," Aunt Fifi said. "They always did, even in Shakespeare's time. Where are you going to do it? And when?"

"We haven't decided. Maybe when Auntie Clare and Uncle Clarence are here, before they go back to Swaziland. And after Mum and Dad and Pin arrive. That way everyone can see it."

"You won't have so much trouble understanding the words once you've been through it a few times," Aunt Fifi said. "How you say it will make sense of it. Merlin would tell you to get your cast to sit around and read it out loud."

"We've already done that," Becca said. "We just thought it would be faster if you helped us, so it was shorter but still made sense."

Aunt Fifi suddenly declared loudly, "Again!"

And with a great swinging blow, she caught Merlin's jeans right off the line with the blade of the axe.

"Look out!" Becca called. The clothespins snapped and before she could stop it, Aunt Fifi had buried the axe's blade and the jeans in a knotty chunk of pine.

"The log didn't split," Aunt Fifi said with disgust. She prided herself on her efficient chopping.

She pulled the axe out of the pine log, and out of Merlin's jeans, too.

"Sad," she said, holding them up. She had cut off a leg. "I told you he should have stopped by to collect his laundry."

*   *   *

"There may be messages more obvious than this, but if so, I don't know what they are," Merlin said, looking at his ruined jeans. "Maybe it's time to give up."

DEIRDRE BAKER

"Don't give up," Becca said. "Maybe Aunt Fifi thinks you'd like shorts. Or maybe she wants to see your legs."

She liked Merlin and thought he would make a good uncle.

"Anyway, we need help with this play," she told him. "I can't get Alicia to be in it. All she does is lie on the beach and grump."

"Do you think something's bothering her, or is it just natural orneriness?"

"She wants an Italian scooter," Becca said.

"Is that so?" Merlin asked, suddenly thoughtful.

He gathered up the rest of his damp clothes.

"'Is not, sir, my doublet as fresh as the first day I wore it?'" he quoted from *The Tempest*, holding up his sea-stiffened shirt.

Becca was surprised at how everydayish Shakespeare was turning out to be. He even talked about laundry.

"It'll be okay if you put it through the wash," she said. "And if you take off the other leg, you'll have a nice pair of cutoffs. And don't worry about Aunt Fifi. When she chops wood she's just really, really ..."

"Enthusiastic?" asked Merlin.

"Yes," said Becca.

"She takes out her hostility in strange ways," Merlin said. "But never mind. It could have been worse. It could have been me she clipped with the axe."

"We were talking about the play," said Becca.

"That would do it. She definitely gets excited about Shakespeare." He smiled. "What were you discussing?"

"How the play's so long," Becca said.

"Shorten it," said Merlin.

"That's what Aunt Fifi said."

"And do a read-through with your cast. Many read-throughs. It will help you figure out what to ditch and what to keep. And it will make more sense that way, too."

"Aunt Fifi said that, too," Becca said.

"See? Sometimes we agree. Even if she thinks bossy old Prospero is marvelous."

"Maybe she just likes magicians," said Becca.

Then Merlin got a call on his pager and had to rush off. "Jane's dad says there's a mystery in their sewage system. Or so he thinks! Off I go for another exciting day in the plumbery. Oh, and here." He handed Becca a brown paper bag. "Replacement oarlocks. Enjoy."

8. Fish for Dinner

It was Aunt Fifi's turn to make dinner.

"What are we going to have?" she complained to Becca, crashing the lunch dishes around in Gran's teeny-weeny sink. "I have no ideas. None!"

"Fifi! Mrs. Barker made that bowl!" Gran cried.

"Well, you should have installed a sink it fit into," said Aunt Fifi. "I may have a word with Merlin about it."

"Leave Merlin be," said Gran. "He's —"

"Let's go to the fish-and-chips place at Diver Cove," Becca said. "Then we won't have to cook. Or shop."

"Yes," said Aunt Fifi. "And Merlin can join us. Should he wish to. And you, too, Jane. You do enough chores around here to deserve a dinner or two."

"We won't have to wash the dishes," said Becca.

"Or try to get Alicia to wash the dishes," said Jane.

"I don't know," said Gran. "Fish and chips aren't healthy. We could have sea-asparagus stir-fry. It's better for growing girls and there's plenty of it out there."

Becca looked out at the sea asparagus that grew on the

beach in front of Gran's. Even as she watched, a border terrier trotted along and lifted its leg there.

"I won't eat it," said Aunt Fifi. "I don't care how many times you or the sea wash it."

"It's just well fertilized," said Gran. "Or we could have lamb's-quarters instead. There's lots of that on the beach. And I spotted some young stinging nettles up by the well. They'd make a good stir-fry, or maybe soup."

"Those nettles were covered with bugs!" said Auntie Meg.

"And we'd have to clean up," said Becca.

"We've done enough chores for the day," Aunt Fifi said.

"For the week!" said Jane.

"For the summer!" Becca said.

"For ever!" Alicia grumped from behind her book.

*   *   *

"I'm glad you thought of fish and chips," Aunt Fifi said, as Becca and Jane piled out of her sporty car.

"Part man, part fish, gave her the idea," said Jane. "Caliban!"

"I'm surprised Gran agreed," said Aunt Fifi. "She hates fried food."

Fried food sounded good to Becca. She was starving. Already the taste of chips, vinegar and salt filled her head. And cod, hot oil and crusty batter.

Or maybe halibut, if Gran didn't mind paying the extra.

"They do have other things," said Jane as they joined the line at the fish-and-chips stand.

It stretched for miles. It was going to be ages before they ate.

"What was I thinking?" said Gran. "Maybe I'll go home and have an oatcake."

"An oatcake isn't dinner," Auntie Meg told her.

"What about the chicken place?" Lucy asked. "You know — in the van by the store?"

"But we're already lined up for fish and chips!" Becca said. Oh, how fussy they all were!

"Is chicken healthier, though?" asked Auntie Meg.

"Not better than oatcakes," said Gran. "Oats have healing properties. They help rebuild tissues."

"But fish is good for the brain, right?" Becca said.

"And what about Merlin?" asked Aunt Fifi. "We invited him to meet us here, and we wouldn't want to stand him up, would we, Mum? After all, he *is* the only plumber on the island."

*   *   *

In Diver Cove there was a bustle of cars, trucks, scooters, boat trailers, bikes, dogs, strollers, gulls and people.

Down in the harbor, there was a bustle of yachts and dinghies, kayaks, paddleboards and fishboats.

It seemed that everyone on and around the island had decided it was a good night to eat out.

"I'm not surprised to see you here, Jane," Merlin said, sneaking in at last to join them. "Given the atmosphere at your house."

"It's a bit stinky," said Jane. "When are you going to fix it?"

"You still haven't solved the mystery in Jane's plumbing?" asked Aunt Fifi.

"Not yet," Merlin confessed.

"Why are you talking so quietly?" Jane asked.

"Why are you all hunched up?" said Becca.

"Never mind," said Merlin, almost whispering. "How's the play going? Have you settled on a date? I thought I'd invite the volunteer firefighters and their families."

"Merlin!" Becca heard then, and suddenly there was Mrs. Barker talking rapidly about replacement filters for her water system.

"I'll look in my workshop," Merlin said. "I should be able to round something up tomorrow."

He turned back to Becca and Jane. "Now, tell me about that eaglet up by Jane's. What happened?"

"It sat there stuck to the tree for the longest time. It wouldn't move!"

"And then stuff dripped on us," Jane said. "Pink and juicy!"

"Pink juice?" Merlin asked, deeply interested, but before Becca or Jane could say more, someone interrupted.

"Oh, here you are!" It was someone Becca didn't know. He stepped close to Merlin. "I heard you were here."

"I'm not sure ..." Merlin said.

"Aren't you Gandalf?" the man asked. "Dumbledore?"

"Merlin."

"Yeah. Hey, I need advice about hooking up cisterns. You can come by tomorrow and take a look. I'm building a place just past the Big Tree."

"Oh, the Big Tree. Well. Best thing is to leave a message on my phone and I'll let you know when I can make it," Merlin said.

"Who is that guy?" he muttered, staring after him. "I've never seen him before in my life."

"You're famous," Becca said.

"I'm just trying to have dinner!" he said.

Lucy had struck up a conversation with the person in front of them.

"Market days it's nuts," the lady said. "I do tons of harvesting the night before, but I have to get up really early to pick lettuce and herbs, and then there's cutting flowers and making bouquets, all in time to start setting up my stall."

"I could pick lettuce," Lucy offered. "And flowers! It would be fun."

"Really? Well, look. My name's Annie. Just ask Merlin. He knows my number," the lady said. "Give me a call if you want to help. We could trade veg and flowers for labor."

The smell of fried fish mingled with the smell of dust and seaweed and creosote from the wharf, and with the sounds of gulls keening, ravens croaking and even the nutcracker chatter of a kingfisher looking for its dinner.

"I'm so hungry," Becca said. "I feel like making eaglet noises."

The line shuffled forward.

Now they were close enough to see the boy who worked at the counter. He was taking orders and delivering fish in a frenzy, making change and even running out to clear tables now and then. He looked like he could use about eight arms, like an octopus.

At last they were only a little way from the head of the line, which was a good thing because now Jane was moaning softly and Becca felt like her whole self was a giant, empty pit burning with hunger.

She felt so hungry she was actually hot inside.

She could barely see the chef working in the back of the cook shack. He was lost in clouds of steam and smoke billowing from the cooker.

And now here came Angharad who worked on the ferry, tapping Merlin on the shoulder.

"Merlin!" she said. "So glad to see you! You know that pump you installed? Something's gumming it up."

Merlin groaned.

"The thing is, could you come by and look at it?" Angharad asked. "The situation's dire."

"All plumbing situations are dire," Merlin said. "Sure. I'll come tomorrow."

"You're a hero," said Angharad. She gave Merlin a kiss on the cheek and was swept away down to the wharf by a crowd of friends.

Merlin was popular, Becca thought, but before she could finish her thought, a great storm burst forth from the side of the cooking shack and there was a terrific shout.

The counter boy disappeared completely, as if he'd been felled at his station.

"No!" Merlin clutched his head.

"It can't possibly be plumbing," Aunt Fifi said.

"Anything can be plumbing," said Merlin.

"We should have had nettles and lamb's-quarters," said Gran.

People at the head of the line were mumbling. The counter boy reappeared as suddenly as he'd disappeared and said something to them.

"The deep fryer's bust!" someone cried out. "But I've been waiting for hours!"

Becca's stomach gave a sad fall.

"I'm sorry to say that the deep fryer is no longer functioning," the counter boy announced. "There will be no more fish or chips for the duration. However, we do serve hamburgers."

"Hamburgers!" Auntie Meg said. "Do we want hamburgers?"

Becca couldn't believe how much discussion could go into such a decision. It was easy. Food or no food? What would the mother eagle say?

It was a no-brainer.

But not for Gran. "Maybe we should go to the chicken place after all," she said.

"What's wrong with hamburgers?" Becca asked.

"What do you think, Meg?" Gran asked. "Hamburgers, or try the chicken van?"

"I've heard the chicken's really good," said Jane.

"Do you want to wait even longer?" muttered Becca.

"But hamburgers sound great," Jane added quickly.

"Well, I don't know," Gran said. "Nettles ..."

"The beef's organic," said Merlin.

"And grown on the island," said Aunt Fifi.

"Why can't they just grill the fish like they do hamburgers?" asked Becca.

"I guess hamburgers are okay," Auntie Meg finally agreed.

"And — oh, no!" said Merlin. "Here comes the marriage commissioner, and I just know she's going to ask me about composting toilets. About which I know nothing!" He bent down and fiddled with his shoe. "Tell me when she's gone, Becca," he begged. "Don't let her see me. Go on, crowd around. You, too, Jane."

In the end, the marriage commissioner wandered down the wharf, and everyone agreed on hamburgers. Or grilled fish, if the chef agreed.

"We shouldn't have stepped out of the line," Becca lamented.

"We'll have to join at the back again," said Jane sadly.

"Look," said Merlin. "Please, just get me some food. I don't care what. I'm going to sit on the beach under a tree with long concealing branches, where no one will find me."

"No," said Gran, glaring at Aunt Fifi.

"I was just going to keep him company," she said.

"We need you to carry hamburgers," said Gran, but Becca couldn't see why. Between herself and Jane, Auntie Meg, Gran, Lucy and Alicia, they had enough hands to carry food for everyone.

She thought Gran's efforts to keep Fifi and Merlin apart were bound to fail.

The sun dropped to the tops of the mountains. Soon they'd be standing in shadow and it wouldn't be so roasting hot. The evening would be almost over and still no dinner.

Auntie Meg and Aunt Fifi had a long talk about cooking. All they seemed to want to think about was food.

Now the chef looked like he was having a temper tantrum. He jumped around by the grill at the side of the cookhouse. He banged on it with his spatula, and the counter boy went over to talk to him.

Lucy came back from exploring the wharf.

"There are boats for sale," she announced. "Sailing dinghies. Don't we have any food yet?"

"No," Becca said. "And we're going to have hamburgers."

"Hamburgers!" Lucy said. "But I've given up red meat!"

At that moment the counter boy made his second announcement.

"I'm awfully sorry," he called out. "Our grill's having trouble keeping up with the customers tonight. It's given up the ghost. All we can serve now is pop and bits of lettuce and tomato. And mustard and vinegar and ketchup in individual packets," he added. "In case that appeals."

"At least it wasn't the plumbing that gave up the ghost," Merlin said when they told him.

*　*　*

"Is there any point in even trying to turn in here?" Aunt Fifi wondered when they got to the parking lot for the chicken van. A steady stream of cars and bicycles was pouring out into the road, turning and disappearing down the now-twilit lane into the cool of the night.

"There's a reason they're all leaving," Jane said. "I just know it."

But it was as if none of them could quite believe it, Becca thought, because every one of them — Auntie Meg and Gran, Lucy and Alicia, Aunt Fifi and Merlin, Jane and even Becca herself — had to be told personally by the chicken man that he was now entirely out of chicken.

He had to tell Jane twice. She thought he might have changed his mind the second time, but he hadn't.

"Oh, Merlin!" the chicken man called after them. "I need to talk to you!"

"I didn't hear that," Merlin said, tossing his van keys to Auntie Meg and jumping into Aunt Fifi's little car with her. "Floor it, Fifi!"

And they zoomed off in a direction entirely wrong for going home to Gran's.

* * *

"There's something wholesome about oatcakes," Gran said, as they sat on their own dark beach eating crackers. "And the lamb's-quarters are tasty. I've never made a salad with them before."

"I feel faint," Jane said. "I think I'll go home. It smells bad there, but as far as I know Mum and Dad have food."

It was like the magical feast that appeared in *The Tempest*, Becca thought. It vanished when the characters tried to eat it. The fish and chips had all been in their heads. They got to think about them and look at them and even smell them.

Then suddenly, they weren't there.

She felt a pang of envy for the eaglet with its raw fish.

9. The Wood Pile

~~~~~~

JANE HAD an eagle-headache.

"They just go on and on," she said. "We need somewhere better than the treehouse to rehearse. And it's not just the eagles. Now we've got the mystery in the plumbing and Merlin's always around and Mum and Dad are always having fits. And I don't mean in a good way."

She thought for a moment.

"Maybe we could practice in the clearing by the beach. Nobody would even see us. And no eagles live there."

"Merlin's brother-in-law dumped Gran's load of wood there," said Becca.

"All the better," said Jane, finishing her toast and marmalade. "Prospero makes Ferdinand carry wood — remember? It can be a prop."

She brushed her crumbs into the salal.

Becca looked at her.

"For the towhee," Jane said. "It's hungry, too."

* * *

The heap of wood and the swooping cedar branches above it hid the actors from the beach. It was perfect — not far from the house and not too near. Peaceful. And nobody ever went there except people delivering wood for Gran.

"Let's start with Act Three, Scene One," said Becca. "Enter Ferdinand, bearing a log. That's what it says."

"Okay!" Jane hefted up a piece of pine.

"'I must remove some thousands of these logs, and pile them up,'" she said, and carried it across the clearing.

"Just drop it there," Becca said. "We can move it back later."

A shower of cones descended from the trees and pattered down on them.

"What was that?" Lucy asked.

"Wind," said Becca. "Dugald says it's going to get blowy."

"That log gave me slivers," Jane said.

"We'll get you work gloves," said Becca.

"Why are you taking your clothes off?" Lucy asked.

"A pine cone fell into my underpants," said Jane, pulling her shorts back up.

"Come on. Get another log," Becca said. "Lucy, look at Ferdinand in a moony way. You're supposed to be crazy about him."

"'If you sit down, I'll bear your logs the while,'" Lucy told Jane, her Ferdinand. She staggered off with her arms full of alder.

"Maybe try to sound more swoony," Becca said.

"I'm not swoony," said Lucy. "Mum says I'm practical-minded."

Another shower of cones fell, and Lucy shook the itchy bits of tree out of her hair.

"Maybe it's a jay," said Jane. "They like picking at cones."

"But there aren't any jays here," said Lucy.

"You don't have to *be* swoony," Becca told Lucy, ignoring the falling cones. "You just have to *sound* swoony. It's acting! Come on — let's start again and go through without interruptions."

"'I must remove some thousands of these logs, and pile them up,'" Jane began again, carting wood.

"Becca!"

And now here was Auntie Meg, tramping through the salal.

"Fifi and I are heading to the farmers' market. Want to come?"

"We're rehearsing," Becca told her.

"Okay!" said Auntie Meg. "Gran's helping Mac and no one knows where Alicia is, so the place is yours."

Lucy wiped sweat off her forehead with the bottom of her T-shirt.

Then Auntie Meg just stood there. For a person going to the farmers' market, she was remarkably stationary.

"'I must remove some thousands of these logs, and pile them up,'" Jane said, yet again.

"'If you sit down, I'll bear your logs,'" Lucy replied, lifting chunks of pine. "Really, we should just use the wheelbarrow," she muttered, stopping to stack the wood they'd moved so it wouldn't fall over. "I've got sap all over my arms now."

"I'm trying to get them to sound like they're in love, and it isn't working," Becca whispered to Auntie Meg.

"Merlin's the expert on that," said Auntie Meg. "Didn't he act a lot of Shakespeare's lovers? But I have to say — when Martin and I were going out we did a lot of chores together. We fell in love tearing down an old boathouse."

She headed off.

Huh, Becca thought. Merlin's complaints about Shakespeare's drippy lovers were starting to make sense to her. Jane's and Lucy's lines were kind of sappy. O most dear mistress. O precious creature.

Or maybe Shakespeare was saying that love wasn't just about swooniness. It was about doing chores together. If so, Jane and Lucy were the best couple ever. Look at all the wood they'd moved in only a few minutes.

They finally finished the scene, and with a thousand thousand farewells, blundered into the salal and evergreen huckleberries.

Lucy bent to pick up the script she'd dropped and without warning, without even a rustle or the snap of a branch, the bushes exploded in her face.

"A-ha-ha-ha! You sound ridiculous!" screeched Alicia, leaping up with her hair full of twigs.

Bam! Her head hit Lucy smack in the middle of the face.

"Ow!" Lucy screamed, and fell like a tree that had been axed, right into the shrubbery.

She lay stock still in the bushes.

"It was an accident!" said Alicia.

"Oh," Lucy said faintly. The glossy salal leaves closed over her face. "I swooned," she murmured from deep in the undergrowth.

"Why are you here?" Becca turned on Alicia. "You don't want to be in the play, so quit tossing pine cones around! Go do whatever you want somewhere else!"

Becca was so mad she stamped her foot. She hadn't done that since she was a baby.

"They aren't pine cones!" Alicia retorted. "They're fir cones. Byeeee!"

"She sounds like she's about two years old!" Becca fumed.

"Or two weeks!" said Jane.

"Two days," Lucy muttered beneath the salal.

No wonder Merlin said acting was dangerous, what with people sneaking in the bushes. What with sabotage!

"We can't go on until you're okay," Becca told Lucy.

"She has to play the drunken jester in the next scene," Jane said. "She can't pass out now."

"Has your mum taught you any first aid, Lucy?" asked Becca.

"Keep me warm, talk to me soothingly, don't let me go to sleep," she said. "Oh — here comes Frank."

Gran's cat started licking Lucy's face. The only part of him Becca could see was his tail, poking out of the salal and twitching.

"It tickles!" Lucy said.

"Frank's reviving you," said Becca.

"I'll be fine," Lucy said. "Besides, I'm almost remembering my lines now."

"Your eyes aren't crossed or anything," Becca said. "And if you can remember your lines maybe you don't have a concussion."

They began the scene again, while Frank shoved his head into Gran's load of wood, his tail quivering like a burgee in a stiff breeze.

"Come on!" Becca urged Lucy and Jane, so that they said their lines extra fast, double-tripping on the log-carrying like ferries on a busy day.

"'But you, O you, so perfect and so peerless,'" cried Jane.

A shadow darted from the wood pile and vanished in the undergrowth.

"'I would not wish any companion in the world but you!'"

Lucy's voice was nothing compared to the ferocious growl that came pouring from Frank at that moment. He filled the air with a roar so savage that Becca's hairs stood on end. She actually felt her skin change, as if she herself was becoming a creature of *The Tempest.*

Frank raced into the salal, screaming with rage and blind, urgent purpose. Branches cracked and leaves whipped with the fury of his passing. Someone, something, ran before him, hissing and screeching and crying out desperately with a voice that, horribly, sounded almost human.

The voices rose in a seething fit of scratch-and-tear argument that seemed as though it must be fatal.

Then suddenly, there was quiet.

"What was that!"

Becca raced after Frank, and Jane and Lucy pounded after her.

But Becca wasn't sure she actually wanted to see whatever would be waiting for her when she caught up with Frank.

He had come to a halt under Gran's house. He was hissing and spitting as he glared up into the regions of wiring and pipes, insulation and subfloor, little lanes and alleyways that he could never fit into.

Whatever it was had run up there, and was safe for now.

"Frank, come away," Becca said. Even to herself, she sounded feeble. She could hardly look at Frank in the same way, now that she'd heard his toothy roar.

"I think I've got palpitations!" Lucy said.

"Oh, man," said Jane. "Something under the house. That's not good news."

"Come away, Frank," Becca repeated. She thought of tempting him with a sardine, but that hardly seemed like enough. He'd sounded ready to tear up a live shark.

"Something's living under there," Jane said. "Let's hope it hasn't got into the plumbing or you'll have Merlin around morning, noon and night."

"We usually do anyway," Becca said. "And Merlin can't be worse than whatever that was."

Whatever it was, it was quiet now, almost as if it had never been.

They went back to the wood pile.

"Should we do the log scene one last time?" Becca wondered.

"I don't have to look at the script at all now," said Jane. "Listen: 'I must remove some thousand of these logs, and pile them up ...'"

Lucy stepped in then, a Miranda who excelled at lugging wood around.

And she was better at being swoony now. Alicia crashing into her face had helped. Even though her nose was slightly swollen.

"'I am a fool to weep at what I am glad of,'" Lucy said. "Sniff, sniff."

Well, a tiny bit better, Becca thought.

Miranda and Ferdinand made their exits into the trees and there was a burst of clapping.

"Hmm," said Gran, stepping into the clearing. "Have Fifi and Merlin seen this?"

"It's *The Tempest,* isn't it?" asked Mac. "I always like a play about weather."

But Gran wasn't interested in talking about the play.

"Now," she said. "What about this woodpile?"

And that's when Becca noticed why Lucy had been slow, so seemingly distracted. She hadn't tossed her logs on the ground any old way. She'd built a woodpile, quite a big one. It was a truly respectable structure, solid and stable. Becca kicked it and it didn't move a millimeter.

"That girl knows how to build a good woodpile," said Gran. "But we can't have it blocking the path. You'll have to move it, and while you're at it, you might as well build it where it should be. Come along and I'll show you."

"I told you your gran would get us doing chores," muttered Jane.

10. Sound Effects

~~~~~~

"LUCY'S FACE got bashed and something made Frank go wild," Becca told Merlin. "Then Gran made us move the wood pile. Plus, Alicia keeps bugging us and we get interrupted all the time and Lucy isn't a great actor. Otherwise, everything's fine."

Merlin hauled tools from his van, preparing for an early-evening onslaught on Jane's family's plumbing.

"Oh, and Jane has gone and kissed a sea anemone," Becca said. "Two of them, actually. An orange one and a green-and-purple one."

Why had Jane done that? Becca wondered. Sea anemones were squishy creatures, and on top of their squishiness they had beautiful frondy tentacles that everyone knew were sting-y and poisonous. When the tide was low and they were out of the water, they folded their fronds inside so they looked like soft, boring lumps.

But the fronds were still in there, tucked away with stinging, sticking, poisonous bits.

"She kissed a sea anemone!" Merlin exclaimed.

"What are you talking about?" Jane muttered, appearing suddenly.

She sounded blurry and stiff-lipped.

"Goodness," said Merlin. "How did it feel?"

"My lips are all buzzy," Jane said. "And sore."

"She got stung," sighed Becca. "She can hardly move her mouth."

"I have to say, that wouldn't have occurred to me even at my most experimental," Merlin marveled.

"I wanted to know what it would be like," said Jane. "They look like little mouths when they're all closed up." She paused as if her lips needed a rest. "It would be good if you had some ideas about our plumbing. I especially would like it if the place smelled better. Can't you fix it?"

"I hope so," Merlin said. He shouldered his burden of equipment. "As for acting, Becca, here's some advice. Try speaking the lines as if you're making them up for the first time, right on the spot. And think about how everything a character says actually changes the way we see the person she's talking to. Acting is a lot about listening."

He trudged off to Jane's cabin.

"Sea anemones," Becca heard him mutter. "Couldn't she have tried kissing a human, at least?"

"Today let's rehearse somewhere not here," said Jane, a muffled-sounding. "Somewhere without a wood pile. where Alicia won't find."

 park?"

rotted up then, still putting the finishing touches
tail.

"The park," she said. At least, that's what it sounded like. She had a bunch of hair doodads between her lips.

"We'll work on the scenes with Caliban and the clowns," Becca said.

"Stephano," said Jane.

"And Drinkulo," said Lucy, flipping her ponytail.

"Trinculo! Trinculo!" Becca corrected her.

They had almost but not quite enough people for those scenes.

But Alicia still refused to do the play.

"I told you," she'd said again only moments before. "I want a scooter, not a boat. And anyway, I'm a teenager. I'm into reading and sleeping."

*   *   *

"'All the infections that the sun sucks up from bogs, fens, flats, on Prosper fall!'" growled Jane as they tromped along.

"I wish I could be Caliban," Lucy said. "Miranda's so gushy."

"We should hurry up," said Becca, "or it's going to get dark before we finish. Especially in the forest."

"It's still light here on the trail," Lucy said.

"And you sound like Merlin," Becca added. "Going on about Shakespeare's lovers being drips. But you get to be Ariel, too, and that's fun."

She tried to hurry them up by walking extra fast.

"Do you think I could paint my body green? Or m fly?"

"Green?" Becca asked. Now that Lucy was all keen on helping Annie the veg lady, was she trying to be a vegetable?

"Come on," said Jane. "Let's run. The rehearsal place I'm thinking of is a long way."

She broke into a trot, and then, when Becca and Lucy started running along with her, upped it to a canter and then a gallop.

"Yes, green," Lucy said, as calm and steady as if she wasn't pounding along like a champion sprinter. "Don't you think Ariel's kind of earthy?"

"Caliban's ... earthy," Becca panted. "Ariel's ... airy."

Something happened in the air then. Becca felt her hair blow up the back of her neck, lifted by a peculiar wind.

"What was that?" asked Jane.

"It was — ow!" Lucy shouted. "Ow! Get off me!"

But whatever it was, was gone.

"It hit me!" she cried. "Run!"

"It was a giant bird!" Becca shouted.

Lucy was going too fast now. Becca and Jane couldn't keep up with her.

That was why Becca saw everything.

She felt another swoosh of air, and a dark, wide presence swooped over her and Jane. It wafted above them and went straight on towards Lucy.

Its spread wings brought a quick twilight over them.

Becca had time to see its gray-and-black markings, its powerful shoulders. She had time to hear the almost silent of air it displaced.

"cy!" she cried.

"Ow!" Lucy screamed, and the bird silently reached for her hair.

"Let go!"

It had her ponytail in its talons. It pulled and tore at it, as if it wanted to root it right out of Lucy's head.

"Ow! Buzz off!" Lucy shrieked, beating around her head with flailing arms.

The bird let go and flew off, but before Becca and Jane could catch up to Lucy, it came around again.

"Hide!" hollered Jane, but again huge barred wings spread over Lucy like a smothering canopy. The bird raked at her and grabbed at her hair with great clawing talons, pulling and tugging as if it was trying to seize Lucy right off the face of the earth.

Becca and Jane sprinted towards her.

"Go away!" Lucy screamed. "Begone!"

An attack! Becca thought. The park had always been peaceful before. Why would something go after Lucy?

Gran's island had no scary attackers she knew of — not humans or bears or cougars, or even the apes or adders or tumbling hedgehogs in Shakespeare's play.

Or did it?

"Get off!" Lucy yelled. *Whack! Whack!* "Get out of here!"

Was Lucy crying?

The great bird banged her in the head once mo͏ then soared upward, disappearing into the forest a͏s never been.

"Are you hurt?" Becca asked. "Oh, Lucy! W

"I don't know!" Lucy wiped her eyes and bent over, panting. Her ponytail flopped over her head as Becca and Jane hugged her.

"It tried to eat your ponytail!"

Lucy pulled the elastic out of her hair and put her fingers to her scalp. They came away dark with blood.

"Look!" she said.

"It's just a bit," said Jane, inspecting Lucy's head.

"A bit!" Lucy exclaimed. "It's enough! I didn't know this forest was so weird!" She sniffed. "It's never been before."

"Why would a bird attack you?" wondered Jane. "What did you do?"

"I didn't do a thing! Ow!" Lucy touched her scalp again. "It's really sore."

She sniffed and wiped her nose with her hand, leaving streaks of blood and nose stuff all over her face.

"Maybe we should go home," said Becca.

"No, we don't have to," Lucy said. "I know we need to rehearse."

"We'll stay together," Becca said, even though that hadn't protected Lucy before.

"We'll cover our heads," said Jane.

She pulled her shirt right up over her ears so her stomach owed, and her face poked out of the neck-hole.

"No more running," said Lucy, wiping her nose on her

s of light from the lowering sun filtered through d lit up the grasses and cobwebs between bars of

"It's spooky," said Lucy. "What if it comes back?"

"We'll be okay here," Jane said, leading them into a clearing. "I think."

The bird had vanished and the forest was quiet, but Lucy kept her shirt over her head.

"'Prospero's spirits hear me,'" Jane began, speaking Caliban's part in a buzzy-lipped growl. "'Lo now, lo, here comes a spirit of his, and to torment me ——'"

For a second Becca felt her eyes change, as if by Jane's words trees, shadows, leaves and pale patches of evening sunlight shifted and became the hedgehogs, apes and urchins she was talking about, and maybe attack birds as well.

Was it because of the way Jane spoke that the forest changed? Or because a bird attacking Lucy had been way too real?

Or because all around them moss glowed with a green light, cedar boughs rustled, and nearby two trees groaned aloud as they rubbed against each other in the wind?

"'This is no fish but an islander that hath lately suffered by a thunderbolt,'" Lucy said now. "That could be me! Struck by a bird bolt!"

"'The spirit torments me! O!'" Jane shrieked.

Becca couldn't help it. Every time the trees muttered in the wind, she jumped.

In the mossy clearing, the three of them acted their parts, argued and sang, danced, hiccuped, fought and fell over.

"What's that noise?" asked Lucy suddenly.

They stopped still and there was a crackle of leaves, whisper of salal bushes.

"Can I hide here with you?" Merlin asked quietly, as invisible beside Becca as the shadow of a tree.

"Hide?"

"Don't tell Jane's dad where I am," Merlin whispered. "I just spent a lot of time on his system, but I'm not sure it's fixed. And he already calls me morning, noon and night."

"If you sorted out what was wrong once and for all, he'd stop calling," said a voice in the twilight. Aunt Fifi was lurking in the trees, too.

"It's okay for you to stay," Becca said. "But —"

"Can we please finish before it's completely night?" Jane asked.

"And before the attack bird finds us again?" asked Lucy.

"Attack bird?" asked Merlin.

Then, *Who-who-who-who-o-o-o-o-o-o-o-o-o-o!* sang a voice quite different from Lucy's or Jane's or Becca's — a singer who, Becca thought, might speak for the forest itself.

"Probably Alicia," Lucy muttered. "She's moved on from fir cones."

Who-who-who-who-o-o-o-o-o!

"We know you're there, Alicia!"

But it didn't make a bit of difference.

Who-who-who-who-o-o-o-o-o-o-o-o-o-o! the voice cried out again.

"'Be not afeard. The isle is full of noises,'" Jane whispered. "'Sounds and sweet airs that give delight and hurt not …'"

From deep in the island came an answering call.

Who-who-who-who-o-o-o-o-o-o-o-o-o!

rippled like sea in wind.

"Oh!" Jane cried. "Look! It's there! It has a baby. Owls!"
Grrrrrrp. Grrrrrrrp.

There in the dark, Becca's eyes began to see them. Paler than night, paler than twilight, the owls were ghosts in the shadows.

"It's a mum and a young one," whispered Becca.

"Or maybe a dad," said Lucy.

"They're watching the play," Jane said.

Again the hoot of the distant, answering owl shivered the dark air, and then Becca could see neither mother nor baby anymore.

* * *

"Oh, my gosh." Alicia's voice sounded suddenly, intruding like daylight into darkness. "Frank was so freaked I had to really squeeze to hold onto him."

"Alicia! What are you doing here? With Frank!"

"Fabulous sound effects," said Merlin.

"Truly," said Aunt Fifi. They sounded as if they were one person waking up from a dream.

"What are you doing here?" Becca asked Alicia. "Did you get attacked?"

"Attacked!" Alicia exclaimed.

"Yes!" Lucy said. "Something tried to eat my head. A bird!"

"Oh!" said Aunt Fifi. "Barred owls!"

"Your ponytail," said Merlin.

"Barred owls go for ponytails," said Aunt Fifi. "Especially runners' ponytails. For some reason to do with ponytails looking like squirrels and bouncing up and down when people run. Or so some people say."

"You were really attacked?" Alicia asked.

Lucy clicked on her headlamp.

"Look! Blood!" she said.

"Is that part of your costume?" Alicia asked, peering at her. "Is it really blood? Oh! There's a huge gouge on your forehead."

"Bard owls?" Becca asked. "A Shakespeare owl?"

"Barred as in with bars or stripes on their feathers," said Aunt Fifi.

"You're kidding, right?" Alicia said. "An owl didn't really attack you."

"What are you doing here, anyway?" Becca said. "You said you wouldn't have anything to do with the play."

"Anyone can walk in the park," said Alicia.

*   *   *

"What did you think?" Becca asked Alicia later, as they brushed their teeth and spit the foam into Gran's herb planter, something they were strictly forbidden to do. "Did you like it?"

"It's more exciting than I thought," said Alicia. "With the owl and everything. But it's too much work. I don't know why they call them plays."

11. Housework

~~~~~~

GRAN HAD decided it was time to get ready for Auntie Clare and Uncle Clarence. Everybody had to help clean the house.

"Never mind," said Aunt Fifi, marching along beside Becca into the morning sea. "It might not take forever."

All around them waves splattered blue and silver and gold into the air, as if they'd been licked by sunlight.

"Maybe it will take forever!" Becca said. "And it's a perfect sunny day. A day for doing things! Not for housework."

*   *   *

Inside, Gran was sitting by the teapot writing.

"We're going to have a day in remembrance of my mother," she said. She was making a list. "We're going to clean this place from top to bottom. My mum was a great housekeeper. She even washed her scrub brushes."

But why? Becca wondered. Why would anyone do that?

"Grandma was a great adventurer," Aunt Fifi said. "Remember that time she was kayaking and rescued the guy off the west coast? And piggybacked him all the way in through the rainforest because he was so weak?"

"Yes, but she was also clean and tidy," said Gran. "And Clare and Clarence are coming and I want the place perfect for them."

Becca knew why. Auntie Clare and Uncle Clarence would only be here for a little while, and then they went back to their work overseas in Swaziland. Mum and Dad had told Becca that many people in African countries were sick with AIDS — sick and dying. Girls and boys, women and men. Teenagers, even, and babies like Becca's sister Pin. Auntie Clare and Uncle Clarence ran a clinic for people with AIDS and worked with different organizations to get medicine for them. And they helped people who were not sick, too — the grandmothers who took care of the children whose parents were sick.

"A clean house will be more cheerful for Clare," said Gran, writing away.

"Auntie Clare doesn't care about clean houses," Becca said. "She cares about people, and her house is always scruffy. Once when I was there a mouse ran across my pillow. Mollie and Ardeth had to come chase it away. And her bread grew fur, right there in the bread box."

"It's nice for people to walk into a clean house," said Gran. "It's welcoming." It was like she hadn't even heard Becca.

"Mum!" said Aunt Fifi. "It's a glorious day! I refuse to spend it mousing around under the beds. And anyway, your mother would hate to be remembered this way. Housework!"

"Fifi," said Gran.

That was all.

Aunt Fifi threw up her hands and stumped off to change out of her bathing suit.

"You each get an area," said Gran. "Meg, you do the kitchen and fridge, and Alicia can clean the windows, and Lucy can do the bathroom."

Auntie Meg was only partly awake, and Lucy and Alicia weren't really awake at all. Maybe that was all for the best, Becca thought.

"But Jane and I have to go to the free store," she said. "To look for costumes. And after today it's closed for three whole days! And we need to have the play all ready so Auntie Clare and Uncle Clarence can see it."

But she might as well have been talking to Frank.

"Maybe in the afternoon," said Gran.

"But our boat!"

Gran looked at her list.

"Fifi, you take the downstairs bedroom and Becca, you do the front and back lofts — everything — bedding aired, floor vacuumed, boxes sorted, clothes tidied. And go through those boxes of books. We'll take the ones you don't want to the free store."

* * *

Cleaning the lofts! On a sunny day! It was no joke, Becca thought, throwing Lucy's filthy T-shirts back into her suitcase.

"Just be glad you aren't scrubbing out the fridge," she heard Auntie Meg say from downstairs. "Is this old mustard or congealed foot ointment, do you think?"

Becca could hear Gran outside.

"Oh, Jane!" Gran called in a welcoming way. "How good to see you! Becca's in the loft. You can go up and help her."

Jane was armed with her backpack and a pair of sturdy runners. "I thought we'd go on an expedition," she said. "I thought I'd escape our stinky house for a day on the beach."

Becca looked at her sadly.

"You can go if you want," she said. "But I can't."

"Why is your family so grumpy today? Except your gran. She's practically jumping for joy."

"Labor is happening," Becca said.

"What are you talking about?" asked Jane.

"I mean, I must remove some thousand of these things and pile them up," Becca said, gesturing at the loft.

The front of the loft was full of mattresses and bedding and looked out over the sea, and the back part looked out over the trees and was where Becca and Lucy and Alicia kept their suitcases.

Gran kept lots of other things in the back loft, too. A bread-maker, a trunk, shells, games, old clothes, photo albums, books, potted plants — some dead, some not yet so — wrapping paper, camping equipment, a microscope, glass specimen jars, a bag of old-fashioned bathing caps, and something that looked like a fossilized sock but was a piece of coral.

And those were only the things Becca could see.

BECCA FAIR AND FOUL

"But ..." Jane said, "the wind's blowing, the sea's rolling in, the tide's rolling out, the sun's shining!"

Becca shook out her sleeping bag.

"You just dumped out half the beach," Jane said.

"Now I'll have to vacuum it up."

"Why's your gran so good at thinking up chores?" Jane asked. Then she gathered up the sleeping bags and took them out to the back deck, where she held them up, one after another, and shook them.

"Lucy must really shovel it in there," she said, looking at the fortification of sand that had fallen from the sleeping bag.

"That's Alicia's," Becca said.

"Does she ever wash her feet?" asked Jane. "Whoa — what's this?"

A small paperback had come flying out of the sleeping bag. Jane held it up.

The Tempest.

"She's thinking about it," she said.

"I want you to vacuum that loft thoroughly." Gran's voice floated up from the front room.

"How do you expect them to do that with a vacuum cleaner held together with duct tape?" came Aunt Fifi's voice.

Becca could hear her crashing around in the back room.

"Why do you have a commercial fishing net in here?" Aunt Fifi demanded. "No, don't bother answering."

Then there was a thump and the sound of something falling over.

"To think I could be hiking on the beach or having a swim with my niece!" Aunt Fifi exclaimed.

Becca heard the door slam.

She and Jane brought the sleeping bags back in. Becca folded hers, shook out her pillow and tipped her mattress so the sand fell off. She crawled to the sides of the loft where the roof came right down to the floor and tidied up the things she found there. There was a good drawing she'd made last year, and a stuffy she'd got from the free store when she was five, and dried-up pens, and tissues — some used and some not — and a book on marine life of the Pacific Northwest, and dustballs the size of moon snails.

"This is the most asinine vacuum cleaner in the world." Aunt Fifi's voice rumbled up from below. "And why do you keep the chainsaw at the foot of your bed?"

Gran didn't answer.

"I know you don't approve of my orneriness but I don't think that means you should torture me with poor cleaning equipment," Aunt Fifi went on. "Oh, a bottle of single malt! Why is that at the foot of your bed? Mum?"

"Forty-one jars," Auntie Meg announced. "Forty-one partly full jars of jams, jellies, nut butters, conserves, chutneys, pickles and relishes. And some with best-before dates from a decade ago."

But Gran must have been out by the shed, making plans for more tidying. She didn't answer.

Behind the mattresses, there were boxes of books.

"My First Visit to the Dentist," Becca read.

"The Care and Feeding of the Offshore Crew," read Jane. "It's advice for cooks who work on freighters."

"Did Gran work on a freighter?" Becca wondered. "Did she feed them stir-fried sea asparagus?"

"Maybe we could get some ideas from it," Jane said, "for when we have our own boat."

"What's this?" Becca asked. *"Muriel's Beautiful Girlhood."* The book fell open in her hand and she started to read from its thick furry pages.

Muriel was a boring person. Becca read on, and Muriel and her friends hosted a tea party. Muriel then prepared to go out for dinner with a young man, and her mother gave her advice.

Becca tried to think about a world in which someone considered this interesting.

As she started to close the book, it fell open at the flyleaf.

For my dear Isobel, she and Jane read in faded writing. *May you grow into womanhood with strength, love and faith. This book meant everything to me when I was your age! From your loving mother on your thirteenth birthday.*

Gran was Isobel. It was Gran's book, and that must be Gran's mum's writing. Becca's great-grandmother.

And Gran turning thirteen.

"What's growing into womanhood?" asked Jane.

"Nobody says that," Becca said. "Now they say *It's Perfectly Normal.*"

"But it doesn't look like it's about bodies," said Jane.

"Maybe it's not," said Becca. "Anyway, womanhood must have been awful if you had to read stories like this."

She opened the book again.

Now Muriel prayed for guidance about which boy she should marry. Should it be the businessman who was a bit rakish and had been known to play billiards? Or should it be the teetotalling farmer who was so kind to his widowed mother, but whose farm was about to be possessed by the bank?

Whoever it was, Muriel was sure to keep a clean house. She was a hard worker, that Muriel.

Becca read a paragraph in which Muriel tidied up the linen closet. *Every noble, sincere person loves truth*, Muriel's mother told her.

"Imagine getting this for your birthday!" Jane exclaimed.

No wonder it didn't have the beat-up look books got when they'd been propped open in front of your lunch or stuffed under your covers.

"Mother, why do you keep potato chips at the foot of your bed?" Aunt Fifi hollered. "Just curious ... and why's your wetsuit in your bedroom?"

There was a pause, but no answer. Where was Gran?

Had Gran's mother been sorry that Gran turned out to be a person who had a wetsuit, but no linen closet?

Why hadn't she given Gran a book on intertidal marine life? Or birds of the Pacific Northwest?

"Hey, I didn't know we had a wood-burning set," Aunt Fifi said, her voice muffled by the sound of the vacuum cleaner.

From the loft, Becca could see Alicia sloshing the front windows with water and soap, and then using a long-handled squeegee to clean it all off. All the sea salt and grime was disappearing, but Alicia looked about ready to bite someone.

Auntie Meg finished washing the kitchen floor and flung open the front door. The sea wind blew through the house, all the way up through the loft and out the sliding doors to the upper deck out the back.

"I finished the bathroom," Lucy said, coming into the front room. "Gran? Can I go now?"

But Gran didn't answer.

Becca looked through Alicia's sparkling windows and out over the beach. There was Gran in her bathing suit and a wet towel, standing in the wind down by Mermaid's Rock, chatting away with Merlin and Kay-next-door. The sea jumped and sparkled in the noonday sun, and kids were making sandcastles down on the sand.

"Let's hurry up," Becca said.

"I want a swim," said Jane.

They bundled the rest of the books into a box for the free store, but Becca couldn't make herself get rid of *Muriel's Beautiful Girlhood*.

Gran! She wasn't acting at all like *Muriel's Beautiful Girlhood* told her she should.

Downstairs, sunlight bounced back from the floors. The blue sea flashing its reflections through the new-washed windows looked like part of the room. Even the pictures on the fridge had been arranged neatly, and when Becca opened the door to get the milk, she was met with orderly emptiness.

It was nicer.

But it was awful bringing about such a state of cleanliness.

And there was something else, too. The cabin had become tidier and tidier, thanks to Auntie Meg, Aunt Fifi, Lucy, Alicia, Jane and Becca.

And Gran giving orders. Making lists. Saying it was in honor of her mother. And spending the morning on the beach. Swimming. Laughing with the neighbors.

Gran was like Prospero. A magician, a director — not like Muriel with her linen closet and all.

She came up from the beach at last.

Becca and Jane showed her *Muriel's Beautiful Girlhood*. She turned the pages.

"It's a book from my mum's era," she said. "It didn't seem suitable for my own daughters —"

A peculiar look came over her face and she snapped the book closed.

"Oh, Alicia!" she said suddenly. "What a good job you've done of the windows! But they're almost too clean. We're going to have trouble with the robin fledglings crashing into them."

Alicia glared at her.

"Work! Work! Work!" she grumbled as she and Becca waited for Gran to leave, then secretly poured the window washing water into the herb planter. "I might as well be in a play!"

"Really?" asked Becca.

"No!" she said.

12. A Dangerous Wind

~~~~~~

LUCY WANTED to fly.

"I don't see why not," she said, wheeling her bike up the trail on her way to help Annie the veg lady. "Maybe I can get back at that nasty owl."

"We'll rig up a zipline," said Jane.

"We've got pulleys and line," Becca said. "But I don't know anything about putting them together."

"Merlin might help," said Aunt Fifi.

"No! It's Shakespeare," said Gran. "He's —"

"I know, I know," said Aunt Fifi.

"We won't let them argue," said Becca. She thought Aunt Fifi and Merlin were getting along quite well.

"Our plumbing might do Merlin in," said Jane. "Not Shakespeare. At least Shakespeare doesn't stink."

*   *   *

Becca and Jane went to recycling and the free store. The free store was all stuff people didn't need any more, organized like a proper store so you could find what you needed, and sometimes things you didn't know you needed. There were lots of things for costumes — ancient swim fins for Caliban's fishy feet, a robe for Prospero, a rainbow-dyed jumpsuit for one of the clowns and silky pantaloons for the king.

Jane found a harnessy kind of underpants thing with buckles and padding.

"Look!" she said. "We can use this for the chair on the zipline."

"A hernia truss?" said Aunt Fifi when they got home and showed her.

"What's a hernia truss?" asked Jane.

Aunt Fifi held up the arrangement of straps, buckles and pads.

"It's a support harness for someone with a hernia," she said.

"What's a hernia?" Becca asked.

"It's when part of someone's intestine bulges through a tear in the stomach muscles. The truss is like super-tight underpants. Holds it all in. And this one's definitely designed for a man," she added, inspecting it.

"Goodness," said Gran. "Well, it might come in handy. I could use it to tie up the pea vines."

They'd also found an extra book of Shakespeare, one that was huge and called *The Complete Works of William Shakespeare*.

"That looks awfully familiar," Aunt Fifi said.

It was glorious. On the cover was a portrait of Shakespeare sucking his cheeks in — perhaps to distract from his triple-sized forehead and wispy soul-patch. The pages were heavy and smooth, creamy to the touch.

Aunt Fifi turned to the title page.

Becca saw handwriting there. Familiar handwriting.

"'For Fiona on her sixteenth birthday,'" Becca read. "'From your loving mum.'"

The date was Aunt Fifi's birthday. The writing was Gran's.

"But Gran hates Shakespeare," said Becca.

"Maybe she didn't always," said Aunt Fifi. She turned the pages and smiled.

"What are you looking at?" asked Gran. "Merlin! What are you doing here?"

"Just double-checking that sewage alarm system," Merlin said. "And what's this I hear about a zipline? Fifi! What are you reading?"

"'If I profane with my unworthiest hand this holy shrine, the gentle sin is this: my lips, two blushing pilgrims, ready stand to smooth that rough touch with a tender —'"

"Fifi, what are you reading?" Gran demanded. "What are you reading to Merlin!"

"My sixteenth birthday present," Aunt Fifi said. "Which you gave away. Very clever, Mum. But even you can't stop the workings of destiny."

"Becca, what's that?" asked Gran.

"I found it at the free store," Becca said.

"Beautiful," said Merlin, reading the inscription. "Imagine you at sixteen! Fearsome!" He laughed and began turning pages, standing in his oil-stained cut-offs, his hands smudged with whatever he'd been doing over at Jane's house.

"*Love's Labour's Lost*," he said. "And here's *The Winter's Tale*, the one with the bear. Now that's a creepy story."

"Yes, isn't it?" Aunt Fifi agreed.

"Fifi!" Gran exclaimed.

She didn't want Aunt Fifi and Merlin to argue. Nor, it seemed, did she want them to agree.

Suddenly, Becca got it. It wasn't Shakespeare Gran hated, it was what Shakespeare might lead to. Would Aunt Fifi and Merlin argue? If they did, Merlin might stomp off and decide never to come near Gran's house and plumbing again.

If they didn't argue … what would that mean? A new uncle person for Becca? One who lived on the island? Or not?

"Come away," she said to Gran. "It's time for tea."

And she took Gran indoors.

Then Becca and Jane stood over the kettle and looked out the window at Aunt Fifi and Merlin. Their heads were bent together over *The Complete Works of William Shakespeare*.

Before Becca's eyes, Aunt Fifi's hands reached up to Merlin's face and pulled it towards her. With one hand Merlin set *William Shakespeare* gently on the deck, and with the other he drew Aunt Fifi to him with a kiss that made Becca's hair prickle on her head.

It was like they wanted their faces to become one face.

And they certainly weren't arguing.

"Whoa," said Jane. "That's nothing like sea anemones."

* * *

After tea, Merlin helped them set up the zipline as if nothing different had happened.

"It's good to have a few special effects," he said. "Makes it more of a show."

Jane wanted the zipline to zig and zag over the stage, but Merlin said that was too complicated.

"We don't want the special effect to be someone braining herself," he said.

Becca felt that with one thing and another, the play already had a lot of special effects.

* * *

"Come on, Becca," Jane said. "It's perfectly normal. You know they're into each other."

Of course Becca knew. But she hadn't thought about the feelings in it, somehow.

Or the way Aunt Fifi and Merlin would melt into each other, almost.

Her heart was noisy just thinking about it.

"Let's go climb on the cliffs," said Jane. "Do something ordinary."

But even the park was restless. The firs and cedars stirred in the breeze, and when Becca and Jane reached the edge of the forest, the leaves of the Garry oaks quivered and shivered like torn sails in a windy blast.

The breeze had been light in Gran's bay, but now Becca looked into the heart of a brilliant, powerful wind. It was blowing the sea into mountains.

Below the bluffs, water foamed and roared, sucking out and pouring in as if it wanted to pull the island into the sea and drown it.

"It's a Qualicum!" cried Jane.

Mac had told them about this local wind. It came from the Pacific Ocean far away on the other side of Vancouver Island, funneling through a valley and tearing like a train into the strait near Gran's island.

It came up fast and fierce.

Now it blew into Becca's head. It rushed in through her mouth and nose, and even through her eyeballs and ears.

Jane laughed.

"My brain is full of air!" she yelled.

Out in the strait, green swells splintered sunlight in their depths and crested into glittering, lacy billows.

Everything was white and silver and light and radiance and motion.

It was a glorious, sunny wind as long as you weren't at sea.

"Look! Is that a boat?"

Becca stopped where she was in the wind-flattened grasses and shaded her eyes.

"They're crazy!" shouted Jane. "Why are they out in this?"

It was a sleek little sloop, one of those boats made for flying. It had come sailing from behind the point as if nothing much was happening.

But before Becca's eyes, the wind hit it a great, smacking blow.

The sloop bowed down. She heeled abruptly — or was she

keeling over for good? She lay her sail to the sea as if she was giving up, as if saying, "Why bother fighting this slamming wind?"

"She's capsizing!" cried Jane.

Was this going to be like the eagle and the fish? But worse?

Becca thought of being dumped by *Gull,* and of what it would be like to be tossed overboard into these rough seas.

She could see sailors scurrying on deck like tiny crabs.

"I hope they have life jackets," said Jane.

"They must!" Becca said. Wouldn't they?

The deck sloped as if it was trying to tip every last sailor into the sea, and rocked with sickening wallows. Becca didn't see how the sloop could stay afloat, bowed down to the seas like that.

"I can't watch," Jane cried, covering her face.

But Becca watched. It was as if she had to.

Then, with startling suddenness, the sloop was no longer lying down and dying, but beating the surges under her. She rode their backs from crest to crest with long, racing leaps.

It was true that *Gull* was slow, but Becca thought she might not want to be in a boat that was going as fast as this one. Why weren't the sails tearing to bits? How could the rigging survive?

The sloop turned into the wind and slowed.

The sails flapped furiously, and for a moment, the only sign of her was the mast and the peak of her mainsail.

Then there she was again, rolling on the surge of the next swell. The sailors stuck to the deck like limpets.

The foresail dropped.

"What are they doing?" Jane asked. "Why don't they just go?"

"They're reefing," said Becca.

The sloop dove again and again in the cliff-like seas. Bit by bit, the sail got smaller and smaller.

What would it be like to be on that boat? Climbing and crashing, sun on sea, blasting wind.

Excitement. Deeper and darker excitement.

Danger.

Much more than *Gull* with a broken oarlock in the shallow water of Gran's bay.

Thank goodness, Becca could see that it wasn't going to be like the eagle and the fish — not this time. But it could be, in a little boat or if you didn't know what you were doing.

The sailors crept aft at last, clinging again to the side rail.

"They're beating across the wind now," said Becca.

"They're going to be okay," said Jane. "I think."

The wind raged. Becca and Jane turned and started to walk the trail over the grassy bluffs and along the cliffs, pushing against the blast. The sloop toiled across galloping swells, came about and crept on once more.

At last its shortened sail no longer caught the light, but vanished from their sight.

"They'll get out of the Qualicum soon," said Jane.

It was a very local wind. You were either in it, or you weren't — it was that simple.

But if you were in it, it wasn't simple at all.

13. Nature Calls

~~~~~~

I⊤ HAD BEEN a long day.

To Becca, it felt like it had been two days.

First, Gran got them to do an errand.

"How about you and Jane go for a nice bike ride and do the shopping for me?" she said.

So they set off for the store, Jane on Mac's rattletrap and Becca on Speed Queen, Gran's heritage three-speed.

But Jane didn't really believe in nice bike rides.

"Let's ride as far and fast as we can with our eyes closed," she said. "Last one to open her eyes wins."

So they rode down the long hill with their eyes closed, and Jane's bike fell apart, and Becca didn't open her eyes until she landed in a ditch full of stinging nettles and wild roses.

But that was all right. Just a lot of scratches and stinging.

All that felt like one kind of day. Fun, but hazardous.

Then suddenly, after they'd done the shopping, it became a totally different kind of day.

"Oh, look!" said Jane. "There's Merlin. Maybe we can put our bikes in his van and get a ride home."

Because now they had the box of groceries, as well as Jane's bike that was in more pieces than a healthy bike should be.

And there was Merlin. Or was it?

All at once, Becca wasn't sure.

He had his arms around a woman Becca had never seen before — someone tall, strong and spiky-haired. He kissed her. He hugged her. The two of them smiled at each other and laughed their heads off.

The unknown woman had her arm around Merlin's shoulders and she looked at him as if she was thrilled to see him, right down to the soles of her elegant biker boots and right out to the tips of her purple hair.

Merlin was waving his arms and talking like it was the most exciting day of his life.

Was this the Merlin who had been kissing Aunt Fifi only the day before? A kiss that had made Becca's hair prickle on her head?

The sad, dropping feeling in her stomach took her by surprise.

"Maybe it's his sister," said Jane.

"He only has one sister," said Becca. "That's not her."

Sailing in a Qualicum would be nothing compared to whatever was going on here. And there was no question of getting a lift from someone as wrapped up with his Friend as Merlin was. Ms. Spiky-hair!

* * *

That night, Becca and Jane crawled into their sleeping bags on Gran's deck long before dark.

It had taken them ages to walk home pushing the bikes. And the milk sprang a leak and seeped out of the backpack and through Jane's shorts and underpants and all the way down her legs into her socks. The raspberries squashed and got all mixed up with the organic fertilizer, and Jane got blisters, and Becca scraped her shins.

But that wasn't what bothered Becca as she stared up through the pine branches at the darkening sky.

"Did he kiss her on the cheek?"

"I didn't see," said Jane.

"What am I going to say to Aunt Fifi?"

Gran would be happy, Becca thought. It would be the end of arguments about Shakespeare.

She couldn't sleep. She tried staring up into the stars, but they only reminded her of Aunt Fifi and Merlin. A star to every wandering bark.

And of the little ship she and Jane had seen, almost drowning in all the storminess and sea spray.

Would the play ever come together? Would they ever get a good sailboat? Would Auntie Meg like *The Tempest*? Would Auntie Clare and Uncle Clarence? Would Mum and Dad and Pin?

Would more bad things happen?

Then her head would fill with Merlin and Ms. Spiky-hair again, and with the look in Aunt Fifi's eyes as she'd drawn Merlin's face towards her.

Who was Merlin's Friend? Not someone he could argue with as well as he did with Aunt Fifi. That wasn't possible.

Then nature called.

Even indoors, out of the starshine, it wasn't wholly dark. Are these my night eyes? Becca wondered, feeling the smooth floor underfoot, and then the cool tiles of the bathroom. The whole space seemed strange after waking up outside. She didn't want to turn on the light and ruin the dimness.

But someone was moving around.

No, some *thing* was moving.

Becca's heart pattered in her chest with a scared, scampering thrum of its own.

"Gran?" she whispered. "Is that you?"

The isle was full of noises, just like Shakespeare said, but she didn't expect to hear them in the bathroom.

It couldn't be otters, surely. Anyway, now she knew what otter language sounded like, and this wasn't it.

There was a murmuring, and a scampering, scrabbling noise. A furniture-moving noise, even.

She didn't flush, so it must have been the sound of her putting the lid down that bothered whatever was so nearby, scrabbling and shuffling. Oh, why hadn't she just gone to the biffy in the safe, comfortable rustling of the forest?

But now whatever it was became noisy and bad-tempered — squabbling and squealing, scraping and crying.

It was awful, like hearing people fight. Every one of Becca's hairs stood on end, even the hairs inside her ears.

Then the noise quieted and went back to murmurings.

Becca put her hands over her heart and escaped back to the deck.

"Where have you been?" murmured Jane.

"There's something funny in the bathroom," Becca whispered.

"What kind of funny?" asked Jane.

"Animal funny," Becca said.

"Otters?" asked Jane.

"No," said Becca.

"Does it smell?" asked Jane.

"No," said Becca, and Jane lay down abruptly and began to snore a little, as if a night without otters or odors was all she needed for a good night's rest.

But Becca lay awake looking up at the slowly vanishing stars, and the tops of the pine trees, and the growing light.

*   *   *

In the morning, she told Gran.

"Something funny in the bathroom?" Gran echoed. "Funny ha-ha or funny peculiar?"

"Definitely peculiar," said Becca.

"What are you talking about?" asked Auntie Meg.

"Animals in the bathroom," Becca said.

"Merlin will have to come," said Aunt Fifi.

Oh! Becca hadn't thought of that. Would he want to, now that Ms. Spiky-hair was on the scene?

"Not again!" said Gran. "And Clare and Clarence arriving soon! Fifi, why do these things happen when you're around?"

"Me!" Aunt Fifi protested.

"We'll eat breakfast at my house," Jane said, pulling Becca away.

"Don't you want a morning swim?" asked Aunt Fifi. "Maybe Merlin will stay for breakfast."

"My mum and dad invited her," Jane said. "We're off."

She threw her sleeping bag over Becca's head and led her up the beach.

"Thanks," Becca said, muffled.

"You looked like a small animal about to be crushed by a boot," Jane said.

"I don't know what I'm going to say to Aunt Fifi," said Becca.

* * *

When Becca got back, Gran was crawling around under the house.

"Merlin said the problem wasn't plumbing," Aunt Fifi told Becca. "He so often says that around here! And Jane's mum called so he had to tootle off. And everyone else has gone to do whatever it is that they're doing — including me."

She took her keys and disappeared.

"What's under there?" Becca asked.

"I have no idea," said Gran.

Her voice was muffled and hollow and emerged from under the house in short bursts.

Frank butted Becca's leg.

"Frank's very interested," Becca said.

"Well he might be," Gran replied, and there was a great ripping, squeaking sound. "Don't worry," she said. "I'm not tearing the house apart. Well, only sort of."

"Do you need help?" Becca asked.

She remembered Frank roaring after the creature that ran under the house.

When Gran finally came out, pushing herself along on her back, she had to cough for a long time.

"We need someone smaller than I am," she said. "Preferably someone with compromised olfactory organs."

"I'm smaller," Becca said. "But what does the other thing mean?"

"Someone with no sense of smell," said Gran.

"Is it worse than otters?" she asked.

"Possibly," said Gran. "It's sort of fishy, but — I find I don't want to describe it."

"My olfactory organs are fine," said Becca.

"That's too bad," said Gran, "but we'll kit you out with a surgical mask."

She made Becca wear an old gardening shirt and gumboots and a toque, and rummaged in the shed for a mask. She held the gardening gloves open and Becca slipped her hands in.

"It must be like this for Aunt Cat," Becca said, "getting ready to operate on someone's heart."

"I surely hope not," said Gran. "In any case, whatever it is lives between the beams and joists under the bathroom floor. It's not about the toilet, so don't worry about that sort of thing. Just clear out as much of the dirt and insulation as you can. Drop it on the ground and we'll get rid of it later. See if you can dig back to where the creature's nesting."

Then she put her own headlamp on Becca's head.

"I don't *think* it's ferocious," Gran said, and went to shut Frank in the cabin.

It was interesting under Gran's house. When her eyes adjusted, Becca gazed up at beams and joists, and white pipes and black pipes leading into the floor. Plywood stretched out around her, and above, where Gran had already pulled some wood away, were the insides of the cabin's underside.

Into the fluffy pink insulation ran a fist-sized hole.

"It's a tunnel," she told Gran.

"Can you get your arm in there?" Gran asked.

"Almost," Becca said. She pulled insulation away.

"The tunnel goes on and on," she reported. She shone the headlamp up.

"Any signs of its species?" asked Gran.

"Something small," said Becca, "or that can make itself small." She thought of the chittering and chattering that had startled her in the night.

It could be a nest where something was having babies. Or where toddler animals were spending their preschool life. It could be the nest of a couple that didn't get along. Of an animal that was at home, or of an animal that was not. Of an animal that was vegetarian, or one that was a raging meat-eater and liked to sink its teeth into the face of anyone who peeked into its nest.

What if it was like one of Prospero's sprites, the ones that were good at pinching, biting, hissing and stabbing?

Whatever it was, no animal she'd ever heard of welcomed someone who was pulling its home apart.

She pulled out more insulation. The tunnel went on, right into the next section of floor, but now she could hear a small, worried murmuring.

"I think it's at home," she called to Gran.

"That makes sense," Gran said. "It's probably nocturnal. Otherwise why would you have heard moving in the night?"

Fine for her to be so calm, Becca thought. She wasn't the one about to have her nose chewed off.

Inside the mask, her face felt damp and itchy. Even though the mask kept dirt and bits of stuff from falling into her mouth, and the toque kept it from falling into her hair, everything about herself felt dirty.

And she wished she had the qualification Gran described — no sense of smell. Now fumes were burning her eyeballs and nostrils. The more she pulled at the tunnel, the stronger the fumes grew. Tea-colored drips trickled and dropped all around her.

It was worse than otters. They only smelled of partly digested fish.

The worried murmuring was now an anxious chatter.

It was true that Becca's arm was smaller than Gran's, but it didn't stretch as far. She kept having to shove herself along in the earth and old leaves under the house, and she could feel dirt trickling into her boots and even down the back of her trousers.

I must be at the end, she thought. The smell can't possibly get worse.

She shone her headlamp into the darkness. She heard *tromp, tromp, tromp*, and Alicia's voice, and water gurgling in the pipe that ran along just beside her ear.

Gran's head appeared, looking under the cabin.

"Alicia's back," she said.

"I'm here," the unknown creature — or creatures — seemed to be saying. And without warning, without alarms or screeches or cries of any kind, a pair of flat, shining eyes glared into Becca's.

Greeny-yellowy eyes, bright in the shine of her headlamp. Sharp pointy teeth bared in her face.

The face Becca saw looked ready to tear her to pieces. This was the creature that Frank had chased under the woodshed. This was the creature that had cried out with blood-freezing rage.

She barely registered the shine of two pairs of smaller eyes. Her mind filled with the sight of teeth as long and sharp as fairy-tale thorns; the red, red wetness of a mouth full of tongue; a bony, dark cavern of throat.

Then she was pushing herself away, scrabbling and scuffling, her breath warm in her mask, her hands muffled in gloves, her head muffled in the toque that shifted and fell into her eyes.

And all the while that hideous stench, the brownish, pungent, blistering drips, and now a squealing, growling scream of sound.

The minks flitted past her like shadows —

"Oh!" she heard Gran exclaim. "Babies!"

* * *

"I've cleaned up animals' homes before," said Gran. "There was a pack rat once ..."

She paused while she handed Becca clean insulation to stuff into the minks' tunnel.

"This is exceptional. Mind you, if you took your time ... a close examination of the debris would reveal a diet of ..."

She fell silent.

"Just think, Mum!" said Aunt Fifi, peering under the house. "If you washed more often this wouldn't have happened! The noise of your feet in the tub would have scared them off."

Becca pushed insulation into the narrow spaces. Under the bathtub, she thought. The stinkiest place in the world.

This had to be worse than any plumbing job.

"What were they doing with babies so late in the season?" Gran wondered.

"I hate mink," said Auntie Meg when Becca finally emerged. "They eat everything — eggs, fish, snakes, hens, mice. Half the time they don't even eat them! They just tear out their guts and leave them!"

Becca thought of the animal bits that had fallen from the insulation. And the tea-colored drips.

"I don't want to know," she said. "I'm going swimming and when I come back no more talking about it."

She washed herself in the sea. She washed every single thing she'd been wearing. She scrubbed her head as hard as she could. She breathed in gallons of sea air and cleaned the foul stink from her lungs, her mouth, her windpipe, her lips, her teeth. She scrubbed her palate with her fingers and swished her mouth out with seawater.

"You're so lucky!" Alicia said when Becca finally emerged. "I wish I'd found a mink's nest. Why do interesting things always happen to you? It isn't fair."

Fair! Becca thought.

But there was this. She hadn't thought about Aunt Fifi, Merlin or Ms. Spiky-hair all morning.

14. The Bear

~~~~~~

"WE STILL need to find somewhere to rehearse," said Jane. "Away from stinky animals and attack birds. Away from chores. I still have slivers from piling wood!"

"And Lucy still has owl scabs all over her head," said Becca.

"Jane!" said Gran. "How are things at your cabin?"

"Something still isn't working. Dad and Mum and Merlin go on and on about the sewage pump and clogged pipes. And the place reeks! It's so boring!"

"Plumbing's never boring," Gran said. "Unfortunately. But if you girls want something fun to do, how about cleaning out the shed? Or chopping kindling? I think you're old enough to learn to do that."

"We have to work on the play," Becca said, although chopping kindling sounded attractive, as chores went. "We have to rush off for a meeting with Shakespeare."

"You could practice the Caliban scenes," said Gran. "There's still plenty of wood to move."

How did Gran know Caliban had to haul wood around?

"I promised Annie the veg lady I'd help her in her garden," said Lucy.

"But what about the play?" Becca asked.

"Next time," Lucy said. "I promise!"

* * *

"We only have a few days," said Becca.

"We'll make a list," Jane said. "We'll put on everything we have to do. Making posters, finding lights, everything."

"Getting Alicia to be Prospero."

"I hope you're right," Jane said. "But I don't know …"

"Practicing and practicing and practicing," said Becca.

Becca knew there was a sandy beach up ahead — a hidden one where they could rehearse without worrying about chores, or aunts who took axes to innocent clothing, or plumbers who showed up morning, noon and night and then kissed complete strangers in the market. A place without grouchy cousins, sad aunts, or Jane's plumbing.

Up near the high-tide line, all sorts of rubbish was tangled in the seaweed. Broken mussel shells, soggy milk cartons, crabs so dead they'd turned white — the debris of humans and the sea. It lay draped in rockweed and snaky kelp stems, poking out of seaweedy mounds that hid warm, salty ooze underneath.

It smelled of the sea and life — a rich, complicated smell that Becca breathed in all the way to her toes.

When they got to the beach, Jane washed her seaweedy feet and Becca found a piece of driftwood for them to lean against. It was comfortable, sort of, and the beach in front of them gradually widened — wet sand, rocks and seaweed glistening as the sea slowly retreated.

It was a good place to rehearse being a shipwrecked king and his noblemen.

Lucy was going to be the king, and Becca was her boring councillor. Jane was one of the treacherous noblemen.

"But we need two of them," Becca said. "They need each other to be treacherous."

"I can play both of them," said Jane. "I'll do it with my hat!"

She turned the brim on her straw hat up.

"Now I'm one traitor."

She tilted the hat and turned the brim down.

"Now I'm the other," she said.

It wasn't just the hat, Becca thought. It was Jane. Her eyes and shoulders changed, and she looked like two completely different people.

In the little bay, the sea heaved quietly, as if it was breathing with sea-sleep. It sent soothing swishes onto the sand.

Becca watched the small waves cream forth, then pull back gently into the sea.

Bubbles formed and disappeared, formed and disappeared again.

The swishes were so soothing that it was a moment before Becca noticed that they were swishing around something on the beach. A big, still mound humped up at the edge of the tide.

What was it?

It was too shapely for a mound of seaweed. Too solid. It rose up higher than the biggest drifts of seaweed and shone darkly with seawater.

Becca jumped up.

"Let's go see."

* * *

"It's a bear!"

"A sad bear," said Jane.

"A dead bear," Becca said.

A bear! On Gran's island!

How had it come to be there?

What had happened to it? It was greatly rotund — swollen, almost. Its fur was thick and dark, except where somehow, on the side of its face, it had all been rubbed away.

There was something terrible and fascinating and wonderful about it. They could look at it all they liked — a bear!

Becca had never seen one so close.

"Its head is so ... triangular," she said. "I didn't know bears' heads were like that."

The bear's legs and paws were stretched out as if it had flopped down to relax on the beach. But, Becca thought, it wasn't relaxed. It was completely — she couldn't even think of a word. Helpless? And so alone! It looked utterly dependent on the kindness of strangers for respectful treatment.

And it had a face. That was bothersome, really.

"It doesn't seem right to leave it on the beach," Becca said, even though part of her wanted to walk away and never come back.

But it was an island. She'd have to come back. And other people would, and dogs, and otters probably, and little kids who might be scared by a dead bear. Or who might poke at it.

She couldn't stand it if that happened.

"We should bury it," she said. "We should give it a decent burial." She looked at the grassy meadow above the beach. Even with all the grass tufting up, you could see rock poking through, sandstone and conglomerate.

"We'd have to take it all the way into the forest," said Jane. "That's miles."

"And anyway, how would we get it up there?" Becca said.

"I don't think we could carry it," said Jane.

And Becca felt somehow that it would be wrong even to touch it, though that didn't make sense.

She put her hands in the pockets of her hoodie as she stood there, and something jingled.

It was the paper bag Merlin had given her so many days ago.

"Oarlocks," she said. "We could bury it at sea."

"If you've got new oarlocks, we could tow it if we rowed out in *Gull*," said Jane.

"We'll have to get help," Becca said. "Some adult to come with us. We aren't allowed to take the boat out by ourselves now. Remember?"

* * *

"Have you been crying?" Alicia asked. "Why do you look so funny? What are you doing with the boat?"

"Just help us," Becca said. She had to stop to wipe her nose on her sleeve.

"But you're not allowed to take the boat out without an adult. Don't tell me you're breaking the rules!"

Alicia suddenly looked immensely pleased with Becca, and she picked up the bow of *Gull* with her strong teenager arms.

"Where are we going?" she asked as they carried *Gull* over the sandstone and down to the sea. "Why do you two look so traumatized?"

"We need an adult. Where is everybody?" Becca asked, as Alicia followed her back up to the shed where Becca collected oars and life jackets and a length of rope, while Jane pulled *Gull* the rest of the way into the water.

"Doing errands, walking in the park, having coffee with Mrs. Barker, babysitting Jane's plumbing. I'm the only one home."

"You'd count as an adult, wouldn't you?" Becca asked. "Come with us. But we'll go even if you don't."

Alicia stared at her. Then, instead of being grumpy or bossy, she climbed into the boat. She didn't even try to be skipper.

Becca rowed. The new oarlocks were fancy bronze fittings with an open Y that the sleeves of the oars fitted into perfectly. Soon enough she heard the comforting chuckle of sea creaming on the bow, even if *Gull* was a gumboot of a boat.

*   *   *

"Are you kidding?" Alicia exclaimed. "That is so cool. A bear! A black bear."

It was still lying there. Well, where else would it be? thought Becca. She must have secretly hoped that it would swim off, by some miracle.

She sniffed a bit, and Alicia looked at her in amazement.

"Oh, Becca. It's perfectly natural. And this bear probably has a couple of brothers and sisters who are out reproducing right now. It's not the end of the family line."

"I don't care about natural," Becca said. "And it's too young — to have brothers and sisters doing that, I mean."

Alicia laughed.

"I guess you're right," she said. "It looks like it's just a kid bear. Not even a teenager! Lucky it. Well, not so lucky, I guess, considering …"

"Why is everything dying?" Becca said. "There are so many dead things this summer!"

"It's only that you're noticing it," said Alicia. "You're going places where you see it."

"Anyway, not everything is dying," said Jane. "The otters are still squirming around, and they have about fifty-seven children. And the barred owls are fine. And the mink family."

Alicia walked all around the bear, eyeing it from every angle.

"It's weird to be so close to it," she said. "I mean, it's a ferocious creature, and it's wild. But it's so not ferocious now."

"I think we should get it off the beach," Becca said. "It shouldn't end up here, just like any old junk."

"We couldn't figure out a way to get it into the woods," said Jane.

"And even if you did, you wouldn't be able to dig a hole deep enough," said Alicia. "When we tried to dig the new biffy, we hit sandstone half a meter down. Remember? And Lucy almost knocked her teeth out with the crowbar?"

"We thought we'd give it a sea burial," said Becca.

She picked up the coil of line they'd stowed in the boat.

"We thought if we looped this around its head or leg we could tow it out and sea-bury it properly."

She didn't want to touch it, though.

"But what if it floats?" asked Jane. "Then it won't really be a sea burial."

"We'll weight it down with something," said Alicia. "Look, you want a knot that will hold tight but slip off when you're ready."

With a piece of driftwood, she propped up one of the bear's legs and pushed the end of the rope under.

"Not a bowline, a slip knot," she said, tying it. "Look at its claws! They're like fingernails, long and curvy and good for scooping up salmon. And that long snout for nosing around in old rotten trees, and for snatching up fish. And the thick, thick fur — usually bears are good swimmers."

Somehow, Alicia talking about the bear so scientifically made everything friendlier.

"Now let's see if we can pull it into the water," Alicia said.

But the bear didn't move.

"It weighs a ton," Alicia said. "I can't believe it floated here."

"We can use wood and lever it into the water," Becca said. "Oh, everything is grim! Eagles drowning and owls attacking and everything!"

"Here," said Jane, and she shoved a driftwood stick under the bear's shoulder and heaved as hard as she could. Inch by inch they shifted the bear back into the sea.

Finally it floated there, its fur fanning out softly, lifting and falling with the sea's quiet breathing. For no reason Becca knew, it floated high in the water like an exceptionally real inflatable swim toy.

"Hmm," said Alicia. Becca could see that Alicia was having thoughts — thoughts of understanding about the condition of the bear, maybe, or about how it came to be floating in the sea.

She made the line fast to the stern of *Gull.*

"Come on," Becca said, and she settled herself at the oars. Jane scrambled into the bow and Alicia sat in the stern, tending to the line. She had brought some rocks into the boat with her, and a tattered hunk of fishing net she'd gleaned from the beach.

Becca rowed right out into the strait — almost to the very place *Gull* had been becalmed not so long ago.

"If we get it out in the current it will drift away, won't it?" Becca asked.

"It should," Alicia said. "And the rocks will help make it a proper sea burial. We don't want it to drift back in and wash up again."

The line stretched out behind *Gull,* and at the end of it the bear floated serenely. Ripples spread in a V behind it, a calm and quiet wake in the sleepy sea. It no longer seemed so sad and alien. They were being friendly towards a fellow creature, that was all. Trying to give her or him a dignified end.

The sea lay around them, and the sky bowed overhead. Astern was Camas Island, the light erect and dependable somehow, even though it was the middle of day and it wasn't flashing.

Alicia wrapped the rocks in the fishing net and tied it securely to the bear.

She said, "You know, there's a service for this. I mean, special prayers for a burial at sea."

But Becca didn't know them, and neither did Jane or Alicia, so in the end, they made their own burial service.

Becca thought about the eagle and the fish.

"Goodbye, bear," she said. "You are still part of life."

"Yes," said Alicia. "You definitely are and we will never forget you."

"O bear, may the deep sea rock you in peace," said Jane.

Alicia loosed the line from the bear's leg, and the bear sank slowly into the green depths.

*   *   *

"Well, that was very interesting," Alicia said, after Becca had rowed them silently back to Gran's bay.

"It was sad," Becca said. "I hate 'nature's-not-fair-or-unfair.' Why can't nature be nice?"

"Neither fair nor foul," said Alicia. "That's what Gran would say, but it's rotten sometimes. The poor bear!"

Becca shipped the oars and pulled out the oarlocks.

"I never knew doing a play would involve so much wild-life," Alicia said.

Then, when they'd carried *Gull* back up the beach, she said, "I guess if you can sea-bury a bear, I can be in *The Tempest*. I don't really care about a boat and I don't think you can earn enough even to get the tiniest used sailing dinghy, and it will all be a lot of work, but I can see that it won't be boring. Probably. What role do you want me to play?"

Becca couldn't believe what she was hearing.

"Prospero," said Jane.

"Prospero! But he's the main guy! A magician."

"Don't you like that?" Becca asked.

Alicia said nothing for a moment.

"I'm honored," she said at last. "I thought you'd want me to be Caliban. Most days that's who I feel like."

Becca looked at her — Alicia, with hair the color of island honey, with freckles and fashionable glasses, muscles from running cross-country and swimming, and a head full of cleverness. Who would have guessed she felt like a Caliban?

"Well, anyway," Becca said. "You are nothing like a fish. Or a man, really, as far as I know. And we already have an excellent Caliban. We need a Prospero."

"And fast," said Jane. "The performance is in a week."

She looked at Becca and smiled.

A miracle had happened.

15. The Kinglet

~~~~~~

IT WAS surprising how well Alicia knew the play.

"I guess the copy at the bottom of her sleeping bag wasn't just warming her toes," muttered Jane.

"Maybe it went into her dreams," said Becca.

It made rehearsals better. And Alicia was a good Prospero.

"She likes to boss," Lucy said.

They decided they'd do the show with scripts, even though they could remember lots of it by heart now.

"I told you it would be too much work," said Alicia.

But it made rehearsals so much easier that Alicia complained.

"The whole reason I said I'd do it is because you were having adventures," she said. "Now nothing's happening but plain old rehearsals."

"Ride your bike down the hill with your eyes closed," said Becca.

"Put your hair in a ponytail and go running in the park," said Jane.

"Maybe I will," said Alicia.

"How's that zipline?" asked Jane.

"It needs work," Lucy said. "And I think I'd better wear a helmet."

"Merlin said he'd finish it today or tomorrow," said Alicia.

"Keep that man away from your aunt and her opinions about Shakespeare," warned Gran.

"I know, I know," said Alicia. "He's the only plumber on the island!"

"We can't risk losing Merlin," Gran insisted.

"Merlin won't let himself be lost," said Lucy.

He might be lost already, Becca thought.

And something was wrong with Auntie Clare, too. She'd been sitting on Mermaid's Rock for hours, and no one was able to cheer her.

Even the tidy house with its sparkling windows, its vases of sweetpeas and roses, lavender and cosmos and bee balm and love-in-a-mist couldn't make her smile.

Becca had seen Auntie Clare's face. Although it looked like she was gazing out to sea, her eyes were closed. Instead of smiling, her mouth drooped. Sometimes it seemed that even her cheeks drooped, as if a sorrow as strong as gravity was pulling every part of her towards the earth.

Becca knew why. It was because of the people Auntie Clare and Uncle Clarence worked with, who were sick and dying. Auntie Clare worried about the grans who brought children to the clinic where she worked, children who came to visit their mums and dads who were sick. How would the grans take care of the kids when their mums and dads died?

"Children preparing for orphanhood," Uncle Clarence had said.

That was the phrase that made Becca forget for a while that she was beached and wanted a boat, and about rehearsals for *The Tempest,* and about Aunt Fifi and Merlin and Ms. Spiky-hair. It made her think about Auntie Meg and Uncle Martin, who would make such a good mum and dad.

Mum and Dad weren't with her, but she knew they'd show up for *The Tempest.* She could always go phone them if she missed them too much. She would feel their hugs again.

What would it be like not to be able to do that?

But even Gran's bony hug couldn't seem to cheer up Auntie Clare, and nor could Becca's hug, or Auntie Meg's or Aunt Fifi's. Even a visit to the barred owls with Alicia and Uncle Clarence didn't tempt her, or a morning swim.

"What are we going to do?" wondered Gran and Auntie Meg, looking towards Mermaid's Rock.

Becca put six heaping spoonfuls of tea in the tea pot and let it steep for an extra long time.

Auntie Clare took milk, so Becca poured some into a mug. She used the biggest mug she could find for Auntie Clare, and a small one for herself. Then she took the two mugs of tea out to Mermaid's Rock.

"It's time for tea," she said.

She put the mug right into Auntie Clare's hand.

Auntie Clare's eyes opened for a moment. "Thank you, Becca."

She sipped her tea. Becca sat snuggled against her and drank her own tea.

"You wouldn't guess it on a calm day like this, but unusual things happen here," she said.

Auntie Clare's face barely twitched, so Becca went on to tell her about being becalmed and then beached by Gran, and about waking in the night and being talked at by otters, and about Lucy being attacked by a barred owl. She didn't tell her about the eagle and the fish or the bear, but she told her about the stubborn eaglet and the mink family under the bathtub, and the little sloop in the big wind.

But even the story of Aunt Fifi chopping up Merlin's jeans didn't make Auntie Clare smile. Then Becca told her about raising money to buy a boat, and about putting on the play and how hard it was to get all the actors together and how many interruptions they'd had.

After a while Auntie Clare said, "I'm going to have to go in."

Becca looked at the giant mug. It was empty.

She took the two empty mugs in one hand, and Auntie Clare's hand in the other.

* * *

Later, Auntie Clare sat on the front deck, and Becca sat with her.

The world grew quiet.

Chickadees and nuthatches foraged in the pines in front of the deck, and ruby-throated hummingbirds sipped at the verbena in the hanging baskets. They buzzed in like giant bumblebees, but very fast.

Even the big birds came looking for food.

"Look," Becca whispered. "A woodpecker."

On the snag in front of the deck an orange-headed wood-pecker made ready to hammer into the rotten wood. It set its beak pounding at the wood like a tiny jackhammer. It made a rapid, hollow knocking noise and then slurped insects out with its long, long tongue.

"Look at that!" said Auntie Clare softly. "I've never been close enough to see a woodpecker's tongue before!"

But the woodpecker must have heard her. It flapped off among the trees and left them in the company of little birds again. Down on the ground a fox sparrow pecked at the crumbs Becca had emptied off her toast plate, and in among the salal stalks the towhee cheeped its lost-sounding *weep-weep*, as if it felt just like Auntie Clare.

"It's peaceful here," said Auntie Clare. "I'm sorry I'm so glum. I hate saying goodbye to women I'll never see again. And to see the grandmothers struggling to take care of their own children's children."

Becca didn't know what to say, so she took Auntie Clare's hand.

"Some things are sad," she said.

At least Auntie Clare wasn't on Mermaid's Rock any more.

"Look at those two flying together," Auntie Clare said after a while.

She and Becca watched a pair of kinglets swoop and dive in perfect unison up and around the trees, curving and lifting.

"They're flying like dancers," Auntie Clare said. "Or lovers! Look at them!"

And just as she exclaimed, the kinglets swooped down towards her, down towards the open door of the cabin and through it, up into the loft and on to the back of the house.

Becca jumped up.

"Where did they go?" She ran inside. "I can't see them!"

She ran through the cabin and up the stairs to the back loft. Auntie Clare followed her.

"Oh, look," said Auntie Clare. "It's trying to get out."

One of the kinglets had flown right through to the back loft and was fluttering up against the skylight. Again and again it flew against the glass, trying to reach the blue sky and treetops beyond.

Becca opened the screen on the sliding doors out to the back deck.

"Maybe we can get it to go out this way," she said.

But the kinglet thought the skylight was the way to get out, even though it was a window that couldn't open.

Becca rattled down the stairs and found the only net on a stick Gran had — a piece of pantyhose on a hoop tied to a bamboo pole. Once it had been a tide-pooling tool, but now it would be a bird-rescuer.

"We should cover the skylight," said Auntie Clare. "As long as it sees the light, it will keep trying to get out that way. We have to make it so the open door is the only light it sees."

"What are you doing?" Aunt Fifi asked.

"Can't talk now," said Auntie Clare, and she thundered down the stairs. "I have to get the ladder."

Moments later she reappeared with the stepladder.

"Watch out for Gran's plaster!" Becca cried.

Bang!

"Ow, Clare," Aunt Fifi said. "Mum'll have a fit when she sees that!"

But Auntie Clare didn't seem to care that she'd bashed a dent in Gran's plaster. She took the ladder straight out to the back deck and called, "Becca, get one of those big blankets from the loft."

Becca ran. Overhead, the anxious kinglet beat against the glass again and again and again.

"Hold the ladder for me," Auntie Clare ordered. "And don't go away. You can let them know if I'm falling off the roof."

"What?" asked Gran, suddenly appearing. "What happened to the plaster?" She and Aunt Fifi stood with Becca at the foot of the ladder and watched Auntie Clare make her way up the roof.

"Oh, Clare, be careful," Gran said.

"Mum, Fifi and I have been running around on this roof since we were ten years old. I think I'll be fine. Becca, pass me the blanket."

Becca climbed the ladder to pass Auntie Clare the blanket. Even from there the roof looked alarming. She couldn't believe Aunt Fifi and Auntie Clare used to run around on it. But Auntie Clare was determined, and bit by bit, her rubber soles steady on the cedar shakes, she crept up to its peak.

She had to flap the blanket a few times. It blew in the wind and she shook it wide with a look of great concentration.

In a few moments, she had spread it over the skylight.

She crept back down the roof, onto the ladder and down to the deck.

"Maybe it will work," she said.

But back in the house the kinglet was still beating against the glass even though it was darkened. And in a puff of breeze, the blanket Auntie Clare had worked so hard to put in place blew back, uncovering a piece of sky.

The kinglet wouldn't stop fluttering up against the window, pecking and scrabbling for the open space on the other side.

"What happened to the other bird?" Becca wondered. "There were two of them."

Auntie Clare didn't say anything. She just seized the pantyhose net and raised it quietly, stealthily towards the frantic kinglet.

"It has wings the color of green olives," Becca said. "Or sort of yellower."

She turned to look again in the loft and there was a quick rush of air like a song past her ears, like a dance by an invisible creature. It was the other kinglet making its way to freedom out the sliding door.

"Well, at least we only have one to worry about now," said Gran. "I don't know how we're going to do this."

"We'll see," Auntie Clare said.

Again and again she moved the net up to the kinglet, but she couldn't catch it. The bird crept up into the sharp angle of the skylight and its frame. It crouched there flapping its wings, trying to be safe from humans and the puzzling barrier to the sky.

Aunt Fifi stood there watching Auntie Clare. Becca had never seen Aunt Fifi's face look quite like that.

"You can do it, fair Clare," she said quietly, and she sat down on the stairs.

Becca sat beside her. She heard Gran talking to Auntie Meg, and she heard Alicia and Uncle Clarence come in from their walk.

Still Auntie Clare kept trying. She moved the pantyhose net this way and that, trying to get it under the bird's feet. It was like it was Auntie Clare against the unfairness of the world or something.

Becca heard Lucy laughing downstairs, and something about Annie's carrots. She heard Gran ask if Lucy would be home for dinner.

But the only thing that seemed important right now was Auntie Clare trying to free the little bird that was struggling to escape.

"I have it," Auntie Clare said, her voice sudden and low. She moved so quickly over to the sliding door and out of it that Becca hardly saw her. Becca and Aunt Fifi stood up of one accord and moved out the door themselves.

Becca saw the tiny kinglet shake its olive-colored wings once and then soar, a swoop that seemed fueled by an instinct much fiercer than the urge to survive. She saw Auntie Clare look out into the empty air, as if its very emptiness was a joy.

"Goodbye, kinglet," Auntie Clare said.

The bamboo pole with its pantyhose net dangled from her hand.

She let out a big breath, opened her arms and hugged Aunt Fifi and Becca.

16. The Tree

~~~~~~

"SHE LET the bird fly free," Becca told Jane. "She actually made it possible for it to fly free."

But it wasn't just about the kinglet flying free. It was about Auntie Clare trying and trying. And about the work she and Uncle Clarence did.

"She does a lot of work with grandmothers," said Becca.

"That's cool," said Jane, looking at her list. "We've got stuff for costumes, but now we have to advertise. At the farmers' market? Fish and chips stand? Ferry dock?"

"The grans look after their grandchildren," Becca explained. "Because the mums and dads are sick."

"Well, your gran hung out with you when your mum was having a baby," said Jane.

"No, I mean really sick." Becca stopped for a moment. "They have AIDS. Some of them are dying. Some are dead already."

"Oh!" Jane stopped eating her toast. "You mean, it's like the eagle and the fish? It's like the bear?"

"Yes," said Becca.

In the top of her mind there were costumes, props, lines, advertising and rehearsals. There was the problem of lighting, of finding time to rehearse when Lucy wasn't with Annie the veg lady.

In the bottom of her mind there was something quite different.

"I thought about it all night," she said. "Nature isn't fair or not fair. But people can try to be fair. And the grans in Africa look after their grandchildren, but they need a way to make a living. So Uncle Clarence and Auntie Clare are part of an organization that helps them do that — get the money they need to set up a business or a garden or something."

Auntie Clare had described it to her.

"So?" Jane asked, munching up her last bits of toast and marmalade.

Bye-bye, speedy new boat, Becca said in her mind. Hello, years and years of lumbering, clumbering *Gull*.

"What if we put on the play to raise money for Auntie Clare's organization?" she asked. "Instead of buying a new boat, we could give the money to them. And it would be for grans. And grandchildren. It would help Auntie Clare's friends. And Auntie Clare, too, maybe."

It would be a bit like seeing the kinglet fly free, she thought. It would be a way to remember Auntie Meg's and Uncle Martin's baby, too, somehow — helping somebody else's, even someone so far away who they didn't know.

Carefully, Jane stood up and brushed her toast crumbs onto the ground.

"It's a good idea," she said. "I don't think the others care about a boat, really. And we could make it donations, not tickets. That would be better."

* * *

After that, the play seemed more serious — or perhaps it was just that Becca felt the day of the performance rushing upon them. The posters were up, and even though they'd decided to use scripts, they'd almost memorized their parts. Lucy's scalp and forehead had mostly healed, and all the tricky changes of roles and costumes were resolved by having Alicia in the cast.

Merlin came by and finished their zipline. He said nothing about Ms. Spiky-hair, but neither did he ask about Aunt Fifi, who was out when he came. He seemed very caught up in Jane's family's plumbing.

* * *

Then came the dress rehearsal, and there were so many problems that Becca felt like sticking her head in the sea to clear her brain.

"It doesn't matter whether it's the dress rehearsal or not," Lucy said that afternoon. "I have a job with Annie and I have to go now to pull carrots and pick zukes and cukes. And then the other stuff early tomorrow morning, and then selling at the farmers' market and packing up in the afternoon. But don't worry — I'll be on Speed Queen so I'll get back in plenty of time."

"It's cutting it tight," said Jane, handing Lucy her helmet. She had woven seaweed into it for when Lucy was playing Ariel, flying on the zipline.

"I'll put posters up at the veg stall," said Lucy. "I'll tell everyone who buys a zucchini or a carrot or a bunch of flowers that they have to come. And anyway, I'll be home in time to dress rehearse the last act."

Jane glued plastic dishes and fake fruit onto the tray Lucy would use when it was time for the magical feast to appear. Becca went to Kay-next-door and borrowed a sheet of metal to use for clashing thunder sound effects. At the last minute, Alicia stormed through the woods and all along the beach looking for the perfect staff for Prospero. Strong and magical looking, she said, but gnarled and seaworn.

Then, when she leaned on it in the middle of rehearsal, it cracked and she fell heavily into the salal.

"I'm fine," she said, emerging with dirt on her face. "I didn't break anything."

Jane choked on a bit of flying moss and got blisters on her toes from the crumbling swim fins she wore as part of her costume.

"I'll cut the foot part of the fins open," she said, wincing. "So I can stick my toes right out."

Becca forgot her lines and missed her entrance, and when Lucy finally showed up, she got all tangled up getting out of her truss on the zipline.

"If you're going to swear it should at least be from Shakespeare," Jane told her. "Insolent noisemaker! Pied ninny!"

Alicia tripped over her own woodpile and scraped her elbow on the slivery logs. Becca stood on her in the darkness and then she herself squashed her face into a prickly evergreen huckleberry bush.

It was a horrible night.

* * *

In the morning, there was a breeze from the northwest and the skies were clear.

The sun slipped up from behind the mountains, and there was Lucy, stuffing her ponytail into her seaweedy helmet.

"I have to leave," she said. "Annie needs help with the last-minute picking."

She was still yawning as she wheeled Speed Queen onto the path through the trees.

"Why can't you get the day off?" Becca asked.

"That would be unprofessional," Lucy protested. "Anyway, I love working for Annie."

She straddled the bike and pedaled slowly up Gran's trail, the seaweed bouncing.

Becca thought of Auntie Clare and Auntie Meg, and her Mum and Dad and Pin arriving, and all the people who would show up to see the play.

It gave her collywobbles, so she ran to get her bathing suit.

The mountains and islands were dark and sharp across the strait, and the water steely with blue and silver flashes.

They would be that way tomorrow, no matter how the play went.

"Best way to begin the day of a performance," said Aunt Fifi, striding into the waves. "Or any day. Come along, you lot."

She dove in.

When they swam back, there was Merlin.

"Here for breakfast again?" asked Gran, sounding not at all welcoming.

Yes, what about Ms. Spiky-hair? Becca thought. Two-timer! Rat!

But then Merlin acted kind, the way he always did.

"I couldn't stay away," he said, "what with one thing and another. And I'm still deeply embroiled in the mystery that is Jane's family's plumbing, more's the pity. But I think we're coming to the end there."

"Never mind," he said when they told him about last night's disasters. "Everything's supposed to go wrong at the dress rehearsal. It's a good sign."

He turned to Becca.

"I thought you might like a hand with the lights."

That would help, Becca thought, and went, dripping as she was, and got the wheelbarrow to collect the lights Mac was lending them.

"Merlin's being very friendly," said Jane in a low voice.

"I know," muttered Becca. "And to Aunt Fifi, too."

"If she's not bothered, why should we be?" Jane wondered.

"She doesn't know!" Becca said. "It's not fair."

But she didn't want to spoil the day of the performance.

Merlin knew all about how lights should show the actors without shining in their faces.

"And the string of fairy lights will be good, too," he said. "Just the right amount of sparkle. And of course you'll have the light of the sea shining through the trees behind you, and the glory of sunset for a while. We'll double-check it all before the performance, when the sun's low in the sky."

Then he looked at Lucy's zipline.

"It's still stable?" he asked. "We don't want anything to happen to her."

He pulled on the line and spent a long time making sure it hadn't loosened.

"Now, anything else you'd like me to do before I head off?" he asked.

"We're okay," Becca said. "But could you put up a few more of our signs?"

"Sure," said Merlin. "I'll put one at the crossroads where everyone can see it. And one near the ferry, too. I have a job over there today."

He drove off.

*   *   *

"We're ready," said Becca at last. "Except for the chairs. And Lucy."

"Where is she?" asked Jane. She was practicing changing costumes fast, so she could go from Caliban to Ferdinand in an eyeblink. And back.

"She'd better be here soon," Alicia said.

She dumped a load of lawn chairs out of the wheelbarrow.

"These are from Mr. and Mrs. Keswick," she said. "And the Henges, and all the people on that side of the bay, and Bill-and-Kay-next-door. We have to take them back when it's over. And you and Jane can get the next load. I'm going for a swim."

It took Becca and Jane ages to collect chairs. Alicia had already been to all the nearby neighbors, so they had to take the wheelbarrow all the way around the corner and down the hill to Dr. and Mrs. Ross's house, and even beyond.

"Where's Lucy?" Becca wondered. "She said she'd be here by now."

"It would be a lot easier if we had three people to do this," said Jane.

She balanced the last chair on the top of the pile. Becca heaved up the barrow handles and they tottered along, the whole load swaying like a top-heavy trailer in a stiff wind.

Jane had to walk with her hand on it to keep it from crashing to the road.

"Oh —!"

The Rosses' chair from the ancient ocean liner *Queen of Constantinople* threatened to jump out on its own.

Of all the chairs they'd borrowed, that was the fanciest. So why had they stuck it on top?

Becca's wrists quivered.

"I can't hold it any longer!"

The barrow keeled over with a crash.

There went a cascade of chairs, right into the stinging nettles by the side of the road. And the Rosses' beautiful teak one on top.

"Oh!" said Jane. She actually kicked the wheelbarrow.

"That sounds almost like Shakespeare," Becca said when Jane had stopped yelling interesting words.

"And besides, a pox on Lucy! May a foul wind blow and blister her all o'er!" Jane finished off. "Where is she?"

Becca sat down in the road to rest.

"Oh," she said. "There she is."

Lucy hove into view like a ship making its way in a difficult sea. A few tired strands of seaweed flopped from her helmet.

Speed Queen's handlebars were hung with bags of stuff, and there was something on the rat-trap, too.

Becca got ready to be seriously annoyed. Lucy should have been in a tearing rush. Instead, she was pedaling so slowly she could have had a little sleep between one push and the next.

Didn't she care about the play?

Then Becca saw her face. Blood oozed from her nose and mouth, dripped off her chin and stained wetly, gorily, down over her favorite T-shirt.

Her favorite T-shirt! The one she chose specially to wear at Annie's vegetable stand. And it would probably never wash clean again!

Lucy was sobbing, crying so that tears streamed down her cheeks, mixed with blood and her runny nose, flowed down her chin and swung by red, stringy strands of nose stuff before they dropped onto her hands, her T-shirt, her knees, her bike and even the road.

"I ran in'oo a 'ree," she said.

She sounded strange, and it wasn't just because she was crying. When she opened her mouth to speak, Becca saw dark nothingness. Nothingness! Where Lucy's front teeth should have been!

"Lucy, where are your teeth?" she asked.

Now she and Jane ran to hold the bike, and Becca saw that Lucy was covered with dirt, with scrapes and scratches. And her mouth looked terrible, all slobbery and bloody, her lips swollen and gashed. And her nose, too!

Lucy said something then, as Jane helped her off Speed Queen.

"What did you say?" Becca asked. "What?"

"In my 'ermos!" Lucy answered with effort.

Becca looked at Jane.

"In her thermos?"

"In my milk." Lucy uttered every word with great slowness and concentration.

Becca was sure she hadn't heard properly. Jane looked at Lucy intently.

"You put your teeth in your thermos with your milk?" she asked.

"Doo dee'!" Lucy said, pointing at her mouth dripping with blood, snot and tears.

"Two teeth?" Jane translated, and Lucy nodded. "In your thermos? Why?"

"Mum," Lucy said, quite clearly.

"We have to take her home," Becca said. "She isn't making sense. Leave the chairs."

"Bring uh wejable!" Lucy said.

But Becca and Jane left Speed Queen and the vegetables with the chairs, all collapsed together in the stinging nettles like the aftermath of a tiny hurricane.

"Just climb into the wheelbarrow," said Becca, helping Lucy, who clutched her thermos like it was a favorite stuffy. "We'll get you home in a jiff."

Nothing mattered but Lucy now.

They pushed the wheelbarrow so fast that strings of Lucy's bloody runoff spattered back with the wind of their going, flicking onto Becca's arms and T-shirt.

And we are not going to capsize this barrow on Gran's bumpy path, Becca thought ferociously, as they fancy-footed their way around the roots and stones at breakneck speed.

"Lucy, what happened to you!" cried Auntie Meg.

"Your teeth!" exclaimed Aunt Fifi. "Oh, Lucy, the play!"

At Aunt Fifi's words, Lucy burst into a noisy, wet storm of crying.

Aunt Fifi was thinking of Merlin, Becca knew, and of the accident that he had told them about once — an accident that had knocked out his teeth and ended his acting career, turning him towards plumbing.

Couldn't Aunt Fifi have said something else?

But Alicia was quite practical.

"Where are her teeth?" she asked.

"In her thermos," Becca said. "In her milk!"

That's what had made Becca think Lucy was really and truly concussed.

"Perfect," Alicia said, reaching for the thermos.

"What do you mean?" asked Jane.

"Milk will keep them fresh and alive," said Alicia.

"How do you know?" Becca asked. "What kind of milk? Two percent or skim?"

"Mum told us once," said Alicia. "We have to get her to the dentist."

"Doo percen'," Lucy mumbled. "I ha'e 'kim."

"The Dental Bus is parked down the road and we're to take her there at once," Gran said, putting down the phone. "Where are my keys?"

"Meg and I will take her," said Auntie Clare. "We may be some time."

They escorted Lucy towards Aunt Fifi's car.

"Make sure you're back in time for the play," Becca said.

Jane looked at her in surprise.

"Bu' I can' 'alk properly wi'ou' 'ee'!" Lucy wailed.

Merlin had said that once, long ago, and it was true. You couldn't talk properly without teeth. Lucy sounded much, much worse than Jane with anemone lips.

"An' I really like uh zipline!" Lucy went on, speaking slowly and carefully even though Auntie Meg and Auntie Clare were hurrying her to the car.

"I'm very sorry, but you probably won't feel like it when you've finished with the dentist," said Aunt Fifi.

"But the play!" Becca said. "Everybody will be here in a couple of hours!"

"What are we going to do?" asked Jane.

"I have no idea," said Becca. "None."

17. Salvage

"THE ROSSES are very nice people," Gran said quickly when she saw the condition of the heritage deck chair. "A few scratches won't bother them. And the tear in the cushion is hardly noticeable."

"I can't believe Lucy brought all these vegetables home after the accident," Alicia said. "This zucchini's the size of a small pig."

Becca could only think of the play.

They set up the chairs. It was four o'clock now. The play would start at eight, but how? What were they going to do about Lucy's roles?

"We could double up," said Jane. "More than we are now."

"Triple up," said Becca. "Quadruple up."

"We could do it with hats," said Jane. "Lots and lots of hats."

"It would make it confusing," said Becca.

"What about Merlin?" Alicia suggested. "He's got all that experience."

Becca thought of something Jane had told her, that all the time Merlin had been working on Jane's family's plumbing, he'd been singing Shakespeare songs and even saying some of the speeches from Shakespeare plays.

But Merlin was a rat.

She thought of Aunt Fifi's *Complete Works of William Shakespeare,* the one Gran had given her.

She thought about how Gran knew things about *The Tempest,* even bits she hadn't seen Becca and Jane rehearse.

"Let's ask Gran," she said.

"Gran?" asked Alicia.

"Lucy's costumes will fit her perfectly," Becca said.

"And afterwards she can use the hernia truss to tie up her pea vines," said Jane.

* * *

"Of course I'll do it," Gran said. "It's a small price to pay for Lucy's excellent woodpile. Just give me the lines."

She didn't hesitate at all, even when she saw all the blood-stains on Lucy's script.

Now Becca stood with Jane in the trees, ready for her entrance, listening to the chatter of the audience as they arranged themselves on chairs and the ground.

Sleepy with painkillers and reclining in the moss, Lucy switched on the lights.

It was time.

* * *

Becca played Miranda and Gran flew through the trees. True, Jane dropped a log on her foot, Alicia stepped on her robe and tore half the seams out, and this time, it was Gran who tripped and fell on her face in the salal.

But she took to Lucy's roles as if they were something she'd always longed to do.

"'To fly, to swim, to dive into the fire, to ride on the curled clouds —'" she cried out, riding the zipline through the airy space between trees and twinkly lights.

The sky darkened. The stars came out and the sea reflected the last pink of sunset into the stage. Shadows of leaves and fir needles wobbled among the actors, giving Prospero and Caliban, Ariel, Ferdinand, Miranda and the clowns a momentary airiness.

"'We are such stuff as dreams are made on,'" proclaimed Alicia, "'and our little lives are rounded with a sleep.'"

Out of the darkness of the audience, Bill-next-door snored — for real! — and everyone laughed.

Gran flew from one side of the stage to the other, her white hair tufting from beneath Lucy's helmet, adorned with fresh seaweed.

"'On the bat's back do I fly,'" she sang out.

"'That's my dainty Ariel!'" Alicia called, and she blew Gran a big kiss.

Who-who-who-whooooo! called the barred owls, and a solitary Pacific tree frog croaked its tenor song.

Out in the sea, a seal slapped at the water with powerful, cracking splashes.

In the audience there was a small commotion as the

Rosses' damaged deck chair collapsed under Mrs. Barker.

"'My dearest love!'" Ferdinand told Miranda, and Uncle Martin and Auntie Meg hugged each other tightly.

Now that it was happening, it was a performance more of amazement than tears, Becca thought, in spite of Lucy's accident, Ms. Spiky-hair, and all the mortal sorrows and natural passions that had inspired it. She hurried to pull on Miranda's dress. Now the play was a magical world, and no longer trouble, worry and labor. In these moments Auntie Meg and Auntie Clare were smiling, and the audience was big, so the takings for grans and orphans would be generous. Up in the trees and out in the sea, creatures swam, flew, rested or nested, each with its own life to live out.

"'Their understanding begins to swell,'" Alicia said, gazing into the darkness of the audience, "'and the approaching tide will shortly fill the reasonable shore that now lies foul and muddy.'"

The tide brimmed in the bay, and up in the trees the Qualicum blew once more, huffing sweet grassy air from the bluffs down into *The Tempest.*

"'We beheld our royal, good and gallant ship,'" Becca declared, returning as the boatswain with his ship safe and sound at the play's end.

It all began with a boat and now it wasn't about a boat at all.

Then she had to rush off to change again.

"'My Ariel, chick … to the elements be free,'" Alicia told Gran, and Gran made one last zip across the stage, and out.

Crash! Becca heard, but it was lost in Alicia's final speech.

In that moment, all the world seemed to be in Alicia. She came near the audience and spoke to each of them — Auntie Meg, Uncle Martin, Auntie Clare and Uncle Clarence, Aunt Cat and Sally who had arrived to take care of Lucy, Mum and Dad and Pin, who had screeched in at the last possible second, Mac, Merlin and Aunt Fifi, Bill-and-Kay-next-door, their grandchildren, the Rosses, Keswicks, Henges, Mrs. Barker and the whole troop of firefighters and first responders, along with Ms. Spiky-hair, Annie from the vegetable stand, the fish-and-chips boy and so many others, Becca could hardly hope to recognize them.

"'Now I lack spirits to enforce, art to enchant,'" Alicia said in a low, serious voice. "'And my ending is despair, unless I be relieved by prayer … As you from crimes would pardoned be, let your indulgence set me free …'"

She stood tall, strong and subdued, and her shimmering cloak drifted to the ground.

*　*　*

In the hush afterwards, Becca felt everything — all the sadness and funniness and awfulness and happiness of the last weeks in a big lump in the middle of her.

Lucy turned out the lights.

Who-who-who-whooooo! the barred owl called once more, and a heron squawked loudly, outraged to be disturbed at his night fishing.

And then, everyone clapped. They clapped, and shouted

and cried and laughed and hooted and clapped some more. There was even some kissing.

In fact, there was quite a lot of kissing. But none of it happened with Merlin's friend Ms. Spiky-hair, who was the very last person to stop clapping.

After the bows, and the curtain calls without any curtains, aunties Meg and Clare and uncles Martin and Clarence brought out piles of food and drink and it became a party.

"No wonder you were too busy to phone," said Mum, putting her arm around Becca.

"Pin loved it," said Dad, and Pin gave Becca a tiny, slobbery kiss.

"Can we get a zipline, too?" Becca heard Kay's grandson ask.

"Becca," said Mac. "You're the magician here. It all started with you!"

"And Jane," said Becca.

Gran gave Becca a hug. "That was just about the best fun I've had in my life. Even if I did hit a tree on that last exit."

"Becca, Jane, Isobel — there's someone new to the island I want you to meet," Merlin said, leading Ms. Spiky-hair towards them. "My Aunt Inanna."

"Your aunt!" Becca exclaimed.

Merlin's spiky-haired aunt! Not a two-timer after all. Becca gave Merlin a great hug herself.

"Inanna has many skills," Merlin said. "Not least of which is that she's a certified plumber."

"What? *Two* plumbers on the island!"

Becca thought Gran might faint with joy.

"Oh," Merlin said. "I guess I didn't tell you. I've decided to go on leave for a while."

"Fifi did this, didn't she?" said Gran. "I knew all this Shakespeare would lead to no good!"

"Now, Isobel," said Merlin. "I do love Fifi and I want to be with her. And I do love Shakespeare. But mostly it was the animal remains in Jane's family's sewage system that were the last straw. That, and being famous. I can't go anywhere without people bugging me! I thought I'd try out a quiet life, so I'm going back to the theater."

Becca thought of Merlin singing Shakespeare songs in *Gull*. Plotting his escape, listening in on rehearsals, thrilled to see his plumber aunt arrive on the island.

Appearing in the park with Aunt Fifi. Jumping into her sporty car and driving off into the night. Showing up for breakfast more days than not.

"I didn't know she was your aunt," she whispered to Merlin. "I thought she was your new girlfriend. "

"A new girlfriend! Never," said Merlin. "'Never, never, never, never, never.'"

Then he added, "That's a quotation from Shakespeare. Fifi is the only one for me."

Never could be sad or good, Becca thought, and this time it was good.

"Is that tattoo a portrait of your favorite drummer or the cross-section of a turnip?" Aunt Fifi said to Inanna.

"Fifi!" cried Gran. "She's the only plumber on the island!"

"She's also a midwife," Merlin said. "And a Scrabble champion."

"Scrabble!" exclaimed Gran.

"Wait!" Becca heard Alicia say to Inanna. "Aren't you the person who came on a scooter? Would you let me ride it?"

"Oh!" said Jane. "It's just like one of Shakespeare's plays where everything turns out right. Only no marrying. Just scooters and Scrabble and plumbers!"

But some things can never be right, Becca thought, looking at Auntie Meg cuddling Pin, and then Auntie Meg and Uncle Martin came over to give Becca a hug and a kiss.

"Thank you," Auntie Meg said, with tears in her eyes. "It was really, really wonderful to laugh. And I'll never forget the sight of my mum on the zipline."

"I told you acting was dangerous," Lucy said to Alicia, her speech muffled with dental apparatus.

"Everything you do is dangerous," said Alicia.

"And now I'm going to have to have root canals," Lucy said. "And I'm only thirteen!" She turned to Becca. "And guess what! The dentist is a sailing instructor."

"Oh!" Merlin said. "How could I forget? I have something for you and Jane —"

And he took them around to where he'd parked his van.

"Angharad who works on the ferry gave it to me in exchange for plumbing," Merlin said. "She said the sea brought it. The ferry crew salvaged it after that last Qualicum."

Becca looked into the dark van at the empty shell of a sailboat.

"'Not rigged, nor tackle, sail, nor mast,'" said Merlin. "Just like the boat they set Prospero adrift in. But you can have it if you'd like."

A boat!

It would be a lot of work, finding the right rigging and tackle, sails, oars and oarlocks. Harder even than getting a whole new boat. It was more like the promise of a boat than a real one.

But it felt like this frail, empty hull had already carried her and Jane a long way, really — from the otters' bedroom to the eagles' nest, from the wild bear to children and grans far away beyond the sea.

Where would it take them next?

Becca could hardly wait to find out.

Acknowledgments

The expertise and experiences of many people and creatures went into Becca's and Jane's adventures. First and foremost, thanks to Ariel and Robin Baker-Gibbs, Lilian Ross-Millard and Christopher and Jacob Ross-Ewart for their island production of *The Tempest*, staged August 16, 2004. In particular, the recollections of Robin, Ariel and Lily have been invaluable. Thanks to Martha Ross, who supported the youthful cast with direction and who was very generous with memories and expertise; to John Millard, who provided musical direction to that summer's *Tempest*, and whose haunting version and recording of "Heave Away, Johnny," from the album *A People's Fame*, echoes throughout *Becca Fair and Foul*. Thanks to Dale Genge and Ian Raffel for tutorials on speaking Shakespeare; to Isaiah Jacobson for being tutored with me; to Robin's grade two teacher Katherine Hunter, who didn't think seven years old was too young for children to enjoy Shakespeare. Thanks to my colleagues Lynne Magnusson, Carol Percy and Paul Stevens for many conversations about *The Tempest*, Shakespeare's language and English in general.

For witting and/or unwitting inspiration, sharing adventures, memories of adventures, or knowledge of matters meteorological, zoological, botanical, marine, dietary, dental, plumbing-related, etc., my debts are abundant. Thanks to Donna Baker, Robin and Ariel Baker-Gibbs, Jenny Balke, Alice Bandoni, Melanie Boulding, Chris Bromige, Paula Courteau, Dennis Dalziel, Doranne Demontigny, Jesse and Robert Demontigny, Robert Gibbs, Jane Harrison, Richard Hiebert, Kathy Hornby, HUGGS (Hornby's United

Grandmothers and Grand Sisters), Laurie and Chris Jacobson, Elias Jacobson, Michele Landsberg, Stephen Lewis, Kay Luney, Giancarlo Moro, Rick Morritt, Hamish Murray, Helen Onorah, Shae and Oakley Rankin, Bill Rapanos, Ilze Raudzins, Donald Ross, Lilian Ross-Millard, Christine Tamburri, John Tayless, Betty Tomoko von Hardenberg, Peter Walford, Cedar Wallace, Ann Zielinski, Amanda and Rob Zielinski, and the deckhand who showed me the dinghy the ferry crew salvaged in Lambert Channel one windy crossing in late August.

Becca, Jane, Lucy and Alicia donate the funds they raise to the Grandmothers to Grandmothers Campaign of the Stephen Lewis Foundation. You can find out more about it at stephenlewisfoundation .org/what-we-do/areas-of-work/grandmothers.

The editions of *The Tempest* used in preparing the story were *The Arden Shakespeare*, ed. Frank Kermode (Methuen, London and New York, 1980) and *The Arden Shakespeare*, ed. Virginia Mason Vaughan and Alden T. Vaughan (Bloomsbury Publishing, London, 2011). Careful readers: note that Becca took theatrical liberty with the sequence of some of the play's speeches. Thanks to Hamish Murray for the gift of *The Wind Came All Ways: A Quest to Understand the Winds, Waves and Weather in the Georgia Basin,* by Owen S. Lange (Environment Canada, Vancouver, 1998).

Heartfelt thanks to Nan Froman, Michael Solomon and all at Groundwood Books, most especially Shelley Tanaka.

Becca Fair and Foul is a memorial to my beloved grandmother, Hazel Haskins, and to the niece we never got to know, Hazel Jacobson. To Bob Baker, Gene Barker and Ann MacKay. To Sheila Barry of Groundwood Books. May they be remembered for blessing.

DEIRDRE BAKER has taught children's literature throughout Canada and the United States, and she currently teaches in the English department at the University of Toronto. She is the co-author (with Ken Setterington) of *A Guide to Canadian Children's Books*, and her Small Print column appears in the *Toronto Star*.

Deirdre lives in Toronto, and she spends her summers on British Columbia's Hornby Island — the setting for *Becca at Sea* and *Becca Fair and Foul*.

Also by Deirdre Baker
Becca at Sea

"One girl's winter, spring and summer of wonder and growth on a glorious northwest coast island."
— *Kirkus*

Becca floated on her back to rest, sneaking peeks at the reefs that were covered with seals ...

From here the seals just looked like a lot of lumps, but she knew what they were like in the water. Sleek and powerful and not really human ...

Suddenly, it felt like she and Lucy and Alicia were all alone ... the water was the seals' home, and she was a visitor here.

"Well, this isn't so bad," Alicia said loudly. "This isn't so terrifying."

At the sound of her voice, dozens of seals poked up their heads. They turned dark eyes and whiskered faces to the girls.

"Just swim," Becca whispered. "And shut up."

★ "… [Baker's] dialogue is true-to-life, witty, and intelligent. Each episode enriches the portrait of Becca's memorable extended family with delightfully preposterous, yet insightful detail … With a lovingly depicted island setting that readers will yearn to visit, this funny, endearing book should find a wide audience."
— *Horn Book*, starred review

★ "This wonderful novel is reminiscent of Lucy Maud Montgomery at her finest — episodic yet energetic, and rich in brilliant characterization and incident … Young readers will be eager for more of this plucky heroine's adventures."
— *Quill & Quire*, starred review

"To call *Becca at Sea* a rite-of-passage novel is to diminish its subtlety. It is really a much richer creature than that, a beautifully paced, perfectly pitched narrative in the voice of a girl caught in the eddy between babyhood and teenage-hood, one that delineates the subtle ripening of self in the midst of fully fleshed family members and friends."
— *Globe and Mail*